BY THE SAME AUTHOR

GREENWITCH

SUSAN COOPER

Aladdin Paperbacks

New York London Toronto Sydney Singapore

First Aladdin Paperbacks edition October 2000

Text copyright © 1997 by Susan Cooper

Aladdin Paperbacks
An imprint of Simon & Schuster
Children's Publishing Division
1230 Avenue of the Americas
New York, NY 10020

Also available in a Margaret K. McElderry Books hardcover edition

Manufactured in the United States of America

16 18 20 19 17

Library of Congress Catalog Card Number: 73-85319
ISBN-13: 978-0-689-30426-2 (hc.)
ISBN-10: 0-689-30426-9 (hc.)

ISBN-13: 978-0-689-84034-0 (Aladdin pbk.)
ISBN-10: 0-689-84034-9 (Aladdin pbk.)
0909 OFF

GREENWITCH

For Kate

When the Dark comes rising, six shall turn it back;
Three from the circle, three from the track;
Wood, bronze, iron; water, fire, stone;
Five will return, and one go alone.

Iron for the birthday, bronze carried long;
Wood from the burning, stone out of song;
Fire in the candle-ring, water from the thaw;
Six Signs the circle, and the grail gone before.

Fire on the mountain shall find the harp of gold;
Played to wake the Sleepers, oldest of the old;
Power from the green witch, lost beneath the sea;
All shall find the light at last, silver on the tree.

GREENWITCH

CHAPTER ONE

ONLY ONE NEWSPAPER CARRIED THE STORY IN DETAIL, UNDER THE headline: TREASURES STOLEN FROM MUSEUM.

Several Celtic works of art were stolen from the British Museum yesterday, one of them worth more than £50,000. Police say that the theft appears to be the result of an intricate and so far baffling plan. No burglar alarms were set off, the showcases involved were undamaged, and no signs have been found of breaking-in.

The missing objects include a gold chalice, three jewelled brooches and a bronze buckle. The chalice, known as the Trewissick Grail, had been acquired by the Museum only last summer, after its dramatic discovery in a Cornish cave by three children. It had been valued at £50,000, but a Museum spokesman said last night that its true value was "incalculable," due to the unique inscriptions on its sides which scholars have so far been unable to decipher.

The spokesman added that the Museum appealed to the thieves not to damage the chalice in any way, and would be offering a substantial reward for its return. "The grail is an extraordinary piece of historical evidence, un-precedented in the whole field of Celtic studies," he said, "and its importance to scholars far exceeds its intrinsic value."

Lord Clare, who is a trustee of the British Museum, said last night that the chalice—

"Oh do come out of that paper, Barney," Simon said irritably. "You've read it fifty times, and anyway it's no help."

"You never know," said his younger brother, folding the newspaper and cramming it into his pocket. "Might be a hidden clue."

"Nothing's hidden," said Jane sadly. "It's all too obvious."

They stood in a dejected row on the shiny floor of the museum gallery, before a central showcase taller than the rows of identical glass cases all round. It was empty, save for a black wooden plinth on which, clearly, something had once been displayed. A neat silver square on the wood was engraved with the words: *Gold chalice of unknown Celtic workmanship, believed sixth century. Found in Trewissick, South Cornwall, and presented by Simon, Jane and Barnabas Drew.*

"All that trouble we had, getting there first," Simon said. "And now they've simply come and lifted it. Mind you, I always thought they might."

Barney said, "The worst part is not being able to tell anyone who did it."

"We could try," Jane said.

Simon looked at her with his head on one side. "Please sir, we can tell you who took the grail, in broad daylight without breaking any locks. It was the powers of the Dark."

"Pop off, sonny," Barney said. "And take your fairy stories with you."

"I suppose you're right," Jane said. She tugged distractedly

4

at her pony-tail. "But if it was the same ones, somebody might at least have seen them. That horrible Mr Hastings—"

"Not a chance. Hastings changes, Great-Uncle Merry said. Don't you remember? He wouldn't have the same name, or the same face. He can be different people, at different times."

"I wonder if Great-Uncle Merry knows," Barney said. "About this." He stared at the glass case, and the small, lonely black plinth inside.

Two elderly ladies in hats came up beside him. One wore a yellow flowerpot, the other a pyramid of pink flowers. "That's where they pinched it from, the attendant said," one told the other. "Fancy! The other cases were over here."

"Tut-tut-tut-tut," said the other lady with relish, and they moved on. Absently Barney watched them go, their footsteps clopping through the high gallery. They paused at a showcase over which a long-legged figure was bending. Barney stiffened. He peered at the figure.

"We've got to do something," Simon said. "Just got to."

Jane said, "But where do we start?"

The tall figure straightened to let the be-hatted ladies approach the glass case. He bent his head courteously, and a mass of wild white hair caught the light.

Simon said, "I don't see how Great-Uncle Merry could know—I mean he isn't even in Britain, is he? Taking that year off from Oxford. Sab—whatsit."

"Sabbatical," Jane said. "In Athens. And not even a card at Christmas."

Barney was holding his breath. Across the gallery, as the crime-loving ladies moved on, the tall white-haired man turned towards a window; his beak-nosed, hollow-eyed profile was unmistakable. Barney let out a howl. "Gumerry!"

Simon and Jane trailed blinking in his wake as he skidded across the floor.

5

"Great-Uncle Merry!"

"Good morning," said the tall man amiably.

"But Mum said you were in Greece!"

"I came back."

"Did you know someone was going to steal the grail?" Jane said.

Her great-uncle arched one white-bristling eyebrow at her, but said nothing.

Barney said simply, "What are we going to do?"

"Get it back," said Great-Uncle Merry.

"I suppose it was them?" Simon said diffidently. "The other side? The Dark?"

"Of course."

"Why did they take the other stuff, the brooches and things?"

"To make it look right," said Jane.

Great-Uncle Merry nodded. "It was effective enough. They took the most valuable pieces. The police will think they were simply after the gold." He looked down at the empty showcase; then his gaze flicked up, and each of the three felt impelled to stare motionless into the deep-set dark eyes, with the light behind them like a cold fire that never went out.

"But I know that they wanted only the grail," Great-Uncle Merry said, "to help them on the way to something else. I know what they intend to do, and I know that they must at all costs be stopped. And I am very much afraid that you three, as the finders, will be needed once more to give help—far sooner than I had expected."

"Shall we?" said Jane slowly.

"Super," said Simon.

Barney said, "Why should they have taken the grail *now*? Does it mean they've found the lost manuscript, the one that explains the cipher written on the sides of the grail?"

"No," said Great-Uncle Merry. "Not yet."

6

"Then why—"

"I can't explain, Barney." He thrust his hands into his pockets and hunched his bony shoulders. "This matter involves Trewissick, and it does involve that manuscript. But it is part of something very much larger as well, something which I may not explain. I can only ask you to trust me, as you all trusted me once before, in another part of the long battle between the Light and the Dark. And to help, if you are sure you feel able to give help, without perhaps ever being able fully to understand what you are about."

Barney said calmly, pushing his tow-coloured forelock out of his eyes: "That's all right."

"Of course we want to help," Simon said eagerly.

Jane said nothing. Her great-uncle put one finger under her chin, tilted her head up and looked at her. "Jane," he said gently. "There is absolutely no reason to involve any of you in this if you are not happy about it."

Jane looked up at the strongly-marked face, thinking how much it looked like one of the fierce statues they had passed on their way through the museum. "You know I'm not scared," she said. "Well, I mean I am a bit, but excited-scared. It's just that if there's going to be any danger to Barney, I feel—I mean, he's going to scream at me, but he is younger than we are and we oughtn't—"

Barney was scarlet. "Jane!"

"It's no good yelling," she said with spirit. "If anything happened to you, we'd be responsible, Simon and me."

"The Dark will not touch any of you," Great-Uncle Merry said quietly. "There will be protection. Don't worry. I promise you that. Nothing that may happen to Barney will harm him."

They smiled at one another.

"*I am not a baby!*" Barney stamped one foot in fury.

"Stop it," said Simon. "Nobody said you were."

7

Great-Uncle Merry said, "When are the Easter holidays, Barney?"

There was a short pause.

"The fifteenth, I think," Barney said grumpily.

"That's right," Jane said. "Simon's start a bit before that, but we all overlap by about a week."

"It's a long way off," Great-Uncle Merry said.

"Too late?" They looked at him anxiously.

"No, I don't think so. . . . Is there anything to prevent the three of you from spending that week with me in Trewissick?"

"No!"

"Nothing!"

"Not really. I was going to a sort of ecology conference, but I can get out of that. . . . ." Simon's voice trailed away, as he thought of the little Cornish village where they had found the grail. Whatever adventure might now follow had begun there, deep inside a cave in the cliffs, over sea and under stone. And at the heart of things now, as he had been then, would always be Great-Uncle Merry, Professor Merriman Lyon, the most mysterious figure in their lives, who in some incomprehensible way was involved with the long struggle for control of the world between the Light and the Dark.

"I'll speak to your parents," his great-uncle said.

"Why Trewissick again?" Jane said. "Will the thieves take the grail there?"

"I think they may."

"Just one week," Barney said, staring pensively at the empty showcase before them. "That's not much for a quest. Will it really be enough?"

"It is not very long," said Great-Uncle Merry. "But it will have to do."

*　　　*　　　*

Will eased a stem of grass out of its sheath and sat down on a rock near the front gate, despondently nibbling. The April sunshine glimmered on the new-green leaves of the lime trees; a thrush somewhere shouted its happy self-echoing song. Lilac and wallflowers scented the morning. Will sighed. They were all very well, these joys of a Buckinghamshire spring, but he would have appreciated them more with someone there to share the Easter holidays. Half his large family still lived at home, but his nearest brother James was away at a Scout camp for the week, and the next in line, Mary, had disappeared to some Welsh relations to recuperate from mumps. The rest were busy with boring older preoccupations. That was the trouble with being the youngest of nine; everyone else seemed to have grown up too fast.

There was one respect in which he, Will Stanton, was far older than any of them, or than any human creature. But only he knew of the great adventure which had shown him, on his eleventh birthday, that he had been born the last of the Old Ones, guardians of the Light, bound by immutable laws to defend the world against the rising Dark. Only he knew— and because he was also an ordinary boy, he was not thinking of it now.

Raq, one of the family dogs, pushed a damp nose into his hand. Will fondled the floppy ears. "A whole week," he said to the dog. "What shall we do? Go fishing?"

The ears twitched, the nose left his hand; stiff and alert, Raq turned towards the road. In a moment or two a taxi drew up outside the gate: not the familiar battered car that served as village taxi, but a shiny professional vehicle from the town three miles away. The man who emerged was small, balding and rather rumpled, wearing a raincoat and carrying a large shapeless holdall. He dismissed the taxi, and stood looking at Will.

Puzzled, Will scrambled up and came to the gate. "Good morning," he said.

The man stood solemn for a moment, then grinned. "You're Will," he said. He had a smooth round face with round eyes, like a clever fish.

"That's right," Will said.

"The youngest Stanton. The seventh son. That's one up on me—I was only the sixth."

His voice was soft and rather husky, with an odd mid-Atlantic accent; the vowels were American, but the intonation was English. Will smiled in polite incomprehension.

"Your father was the seventh in that family," the man in the raincoat said. He grinned again, his round eyes crinkling at the corners, and held out his hand. "Hi. I'm your Uncle Bill."

"Well I'm blowed!" said Will. He shook the hand. Uncle Bill. His namesake. His father's favourite brother, who had gone off to America years and years ago and set up some sort of successful business—pottery, wasn't it? Will did not remember ever having seen him before; he was sent a Christmas present each year by this unknown Uncle Bill, who was also his god-father, and he wrote a chatty letter of thanks annually as a result, but the letters had never had a reply.

"You've grown some," said Uncle Bill as they walked to the house. "Last time we met, you were a little scrawny bawling thing in a crib."

"You sound like an American," Will said.

"No wonder," said Uncle Bill. "I've been one for the last ten years."

"You never answered my Christmas letters."

"Did that bother you?"

"No, not really."

They both laughed, and Will decided that this uncle was all right. Then they were in the house, and his father was coming downstairs; pausing, with an incredulous blankness in his face.

"*Billy!*"

"Roger!"

"My God," said Will's father, "what's happened to your hair?"

Reunions with long-lost relatives take time, especially in large families. They were at it for hours. Will quite forgot that he had been gloomy over the absence of companions. By lunchtime he had learned that his Uncle Bill and Aunt Fran were in Britain to visit the Staffordshire potteries and the china-clay district of Cornwall, where they had business of some complex Anglo-American kind. He had heard all about their two grown-up children, who seemed to be contemporaries of his eldest brother Stephen, and he had been told rather more than he really wanted to know about the state of Ohio and the china-making trade. Uncle Bill was clearly prosperous, but this seemed to be only his second trip to Britain since he had emigrated more than twenty years before. Will liked his twinkling round eyes and laconic husky voice. He was just feeling that the prospects for his week's holiday had greatly improved when he found that Uncle Bill was staying only one night, on his way from a business trip to London, and travelling on to Cornwall the next day to join his wife. His spirits drooped again.

"Friend of mine's picking me up, and we're driving down. But I tell you what, Frannie and I'll come and spend a few days on our way back to the States. If you'll have us, that is."

"I should hope so," said Will's mother. "After ten years and about three letters, my lad, you don't get away with one mouldy twenty-four hours."

"He sent me presents," Will said. "Every Christmas."

Uncle Bill grinned at him. "Alice," he said suddenly to Mrs Stanton, "since Will's out of school this week, and not too busy, why don't you let me take him to Cornwall for the holiday? I could put him on a train back at the end of the week. We've rented a place with far more space than we need. And this friend of mine has a couple of nephews coming down, about Will's age, I believe."

Will made a strangled whooping sound, and looked anxiously at his parents. Frowning gravely, they began a predictable duet.

"Well, that's really very good of—"

"If you're sure he won't be—"

"He'd certainly love to—"

"If Frannie wouldn't—"

Uncle Bill winked at Will. Will went upstairs and began to pack his knapsack. He put in five pairs of socks, five changes of underwear, six shirts, a pullover and a sweater, two pairs of shorts, and a flashlight. Then he remembered that his uncle was not leaving until the next day, but there seemed no point in unpacking. He went downstairs, the knapsack bouncing on his back like an overblown football.

His mother said, "Well, Will, if you'd really like to—Oh."

"Good-by, Will," said his father.

Uncle Bill chuckled. "Excuse me," he said. "If I might borrow your phone—"

"I'll show you." Will led him out into the hall. "It's not too much, is it?" he said, looking doubtfully at the bulging knapsack.

"That's fine." His uncle was dialling. "Hallo? Hallo, Merry. Everything okay? Good. Just one thing. I'm bringing my youngest nephew with me for a week. He doesn't have much luggage"—he grinned at Will—"but I just thought I'd make sure you weren't driving some cute little two-seater. . . . Ha-ha. No, not really in character . . . okay, great, see you tomorrow." He hung up.

"All right, buddy," he said to Will. "We leave at nine in the morning. That suit you, Alice?" Mrs Stanton was crossing the hall with the tea-tray.

"Splendid," she said.

Since the beginning of the telephone call, Will had been standing very still. "Merry?" he said slowly. "That's an unusual name."

"It is, isn't it?" said his uncle. "Unusual guy, too. Teaches at Oxford. Brilliant brain, but I guess you'd call him kind of odd— very shy, hates meeting people. He's very reliable, though," he added hastily to Mrs Stanton. "And a great driver."

"Whatever's the matter, Will?" said his mother. "You look as though you'd seen a ghost. Is anything wrong?"

"Nothing," said Will. "Oh no. Nothing at all."

*   *   *

Simon, Jane and Barney struggled out of St Austell station beneath a clutter of suitcases, paper bags, raincoats and paperbacks. The crowd from the London train was dwindling about them, swallowed by cars, buses, taxis.

"He did say he'd meet us here, didn't he?"

" 'Course he did."

"I can't see him."

"He's a bit late, that's all."

"Great-Uncle Merry is never late."

"We ought to find out where the Trewissick bus goes from, just in case."

"No, there he is, I see him. I told you he was never late." Barney jumped up and down, waving. Then he paused. "But he's not on his own. There's a man with him." A faint note of outrage crept into his voice. "And a *boy*."

*   *   *

A car hooted peremptorily once, twice, three times outside the Stantons' house.

"Here we go," said Uncle Bill, seizing his holdall and Will's knapsack.

Will hastily kissed his parents good-by, staggering under the enormous bag of sandwiches, thermos flasks and cold drinks that his mother dumped into his arms.

"Behave yourself," she said.

"I don't suppose Merry will get out of the car," said Bill to her as they trooped down the drive. "Very shy character, pay no attention. But he's a good friend. You'll like him, Will."

Will said, "I'm sure I shall."

At the end of the drive, an enormous elderly Daimler stood waiting.

"Well well," said Will's father respectfully.

"And I was worrying about space!" said Bill. "I might have known he'd drive something like this. Well, good-by, people. Here, Will, you can get in front."

In a flurry of farewells they climbed into the dignified car; a large muffler-wrapped figure sat hunched at the wheel, topped by a terrible hairy brown cap.

"Merry," said Uncle Bill as they moved off, "this is my nephew and godson. Will Stanton, Merriman Lyon."

The driver tossed aside his dreadful cap, and a mop of white hair sprang into shaggy freedom. Shadowed dark eyes glanced sideways at Will out of an arrogant, hawk-nosed profile.

"*Greetings, Old One*," said a familiar voice into Will's mind.

"*It's marvellous to see you*," Will said silently, happily.

"Good morning, Will Stanton," Merriman said.

"How do you do, sir," said Will.

*   *   *

There was considerable conversation on the drive from Buckinghamshire to Cornwall, particularly after the picnic

14

lunch, when Will's uncle fell asleep and slumbered peacefully all the rest of the way.

Will said at last: "And Simon and Jane and Barney have no idea at all that the Dark timed its theft of the grail to match the making of the Greenwitch?"

"They have never heard of the Greenwitch," Merriman said. "You will have the privilege of telling them. Casually, of course."

"Hmm," Will said. He was thinking of something else. "I'd feel a lot happier if only we knew what shape the Dark will take."

"An old problem. With no solution." Merriman glanced sideways at him, with one bristly white eyebrow raised. "We have only to wait and see. And I think we shall not wait for long. . . ."

Fairly late in the afternoon, the Daimler hummed its noble way into the forecourt of the railway station at St Austell, in Cornwall. Standing in a small pool of luggage Will saw a boy a little older than himself, wearing a school blazer and an air of self-conscious authority; a girl about the same height, with long hair tied in a pony-tail, and a worried expression; and a small boy with a mass of blond, almost white hair, sitting placidly on a suitcase watching their approach.

"*If they are to know nothing about me,*" he said to Merriman in the Old Ones' speech of the mind, "*they will dislike me extremely, I think.*"

"*That may very well be true,*" said Merriman. "*But not one of us has any feelings that are of the least consequence, compared to the urgency of this quest.*"

Will sighed. "*Watch for the Greenwitch,*" he said.

CHAPTER TWO

"I THOUGHT WE'D PUT YOU IN HERE, JANE," MERRIMAN SAID, opening a bedroom door and carefully stooping to go through. "Very small, but the view's good."

"Oh!" said Jane in delight. The room was painted white, with gay yellow curtains, and a yellow quilt on the bed. The ceiling sloped down so that the wall on one side was only half the height of the wall on the other, and there was space only for a bed, a dressing-table and a chair. But the little room seemed full of sunshine, even though the sky outside the curtains was grey. Jane stood looking out, while her great-uncle went on to show the boys their room, and she thought that the picture she could see from the window was the best thing of all.

She was high up on the side of the harbour, overlooking the boats and jetties, the wharf piled with boxes and lobster-pots, and the little canning factory. All the life of the busy harbour was thrumming there below her, and out to the left, beyond the harbour wall and the dark arm of land called Kemare Head, lay the sea. It was a grey sea now, speckled with white. Jane's gaze moved in again from the flat ocean horizon, and she looked straight across to the sloping road on the opposite side of the harbour, and saw the tall narrow house in which they had stayed the summer before. The Grey House. Everything had begun there.

Simon tapped on the door and put his head round. "Hey, that's a super view you've got. Ours hasn't any, but it's a nice room, all long and skinny."

"Like a coffin," said Barney in a hollow voice, behind the door.

Jane giggled. "Come on in, look at the Grey House over there. I wonder if we'll meet Captain Thing, the one Gumerry rented it from?"

"Toms," Barney said. "Captain Toms. And I want to see Rufus, I hope he remembers me. Dogs do have good memories, don't they?"

"Try walking through Captain Toms' door and you'll find out," said Simon. "If Rufus bites you, dogs don't have good memories."

"Very funny."

"What's that?" Jane said suddenly. "Hush!"

They stood in a silence broken only by the sounds of cars and sea gulls, overlaid by the murmur of the sea. Then they heard a faint tapping sound.

"It's on the other side of that wall! What is it?"

"Sounds like a sort of pattern. I think it's Morse. Who knows Morse?"

"I don't," Jane said. "You should have been a Boy Scout."

"We were supposed to learn it last year at school," Barney said hesitantly. "But I don't . . . wait a minute. That's a D . . . don't know that one . . . E . . . er . . . W . . . and S, that's easy. There it goes again. What on earth—?"

"Drews," Simon said suddenly. "Someone's tapping 'Drews.' Calling us."

"It's that boy," said Jane. "The house is two cottages joined together, so he must have the exact same room as this one, on the other side of the wall."

"Stanton," said Barney.

"That's right. Will Stanton. Tap back to him, Barney."

"No," Barney said.

Jane stared at him. His long yellow-white hair had fallen sideways, masking his face, but she could see the lower lip jutting mulishly in a way she knew well.

"Whyever not?"

"He's stopped now," Barney said evasively.

"But there's no harm in being friendly."

"Well. No. Well. Oh, I don't know . . . he's a nuisance. I don't see why Great-Uncle Merry let him come. How can we find out how to get the grail back with some strange kid hanging round?"

"Great-Uncle Merry probably couldn't get rid of him," Jane said. She tugged her hair loose and took a comb from her pocket. "I mean, it's his friend Mr Stanton who's renting the cottages, and Will's Mr Stanton's nephew. So that's that, isn't it?"

"We can get rid of him easily enough," Simon said confidently. "Or keep him away. He'll soon find out he's not wanted, he looks fairly quick on the uptake."

"Well, we can at least be polite," said Jane. "Starting now—it's suppertime in a few minutes."

"Of course," Simon said blandly. "Of course."

*   *   *

"It's a marvellous place," Will said, glowing. "I can see right over the harbour from my room. Who do the cottages belong to?"

"A fisherman called Penhallow," said his uncle. "Friend of

Merry's. They must have been in the family for a while, judging by that." He waved at a large yellowed photograph over the fireplace, ornately framed, showing a solemn-looking Victorian gentleman in stiff collar and dark suit. "Mr Penhallow's granddaddy, I'm told. But the cottages are modernized, of course. They can be let either separately or together—we took both when Merry decided to invite the Drew kids. We'll all eat in here together."

He waved at the cheerful room, a pattern of bookcases and armchairs and lamps, very new and very old, with a large solid table and eight dignified high-backed chairs.

"Have you known Mr Lyon a long time?" Will said curiously.

"Year or two," Bill Stanton said, stretching in his armchair, ice clinking in a glass in his hand. "Met him in Jamaica, didn't we, Fran? We were on holiday—I never did find out whether Merry was vacationing or working."

"Working," said his wife, busy setting the table. She was calm and fair, a tall, slow-moving person: not at all what Will had expected from an American. "On some government survey. He's a professor at Oxford University," she said reverently to Will. "A very very clever man. And such a sweetie—he came all the way to Ohio to spend a few days with us last fall, when he was over giving a lecture at Yale."

"Ah," said Will thoughtfully. He was prevented from asking more questions by a sudden noise from the wall beside him. A large wooden door swung open, narrowly missing his back, revealing Merriman in the act of closing another identical door beyond it.

"This is where the two cottages connect," Merriman said, looking down at Will's surprise with a faint grin. "They lock both doors if the two are let separately."

"Supper won't be long," said Fran Stanton in her soft drawl. As she spoke, a small stout lady with a grey knot of hair came into the room behind her, bearing a tray rattling with cups and plates.

"Evenin', Perfessor," she said, beaming at Merriman. Will liked her face instantly: all its lines seemed carved by smiling.

"Evening, Mrs Penhallow."

"Will," said his uncle, "this is Mrs Penhallow. She and her husband own these cottages. My nephew Will."

She smiled at him, setting down the tray. "Welcome to Trewissick, m'dear. We'll make sure you do have a wonderful holiday, with those other three scallywags."

"Thank you," Will said.

The dividing door burst open, and the three Drews came piling in.

"Mrs Penhallow! How are you?"

"Have you seen Rufus about?"

"Will Mr Penhallow take us fishing this time?"

"Is that awful Mrs Palk still here? Or her nephew?"

"How's the *White Heather*?"

"Slowly, slowly," she said, laughing.

"Well," Barney said. "How's Mr Penhallow?"

"He'm fine. Out on the boat now, o' course. Now you just bide a moment while I get your supper." She bustled out.

"I can see you three know your way about the place," said Bill Stanton, his round face solemn.

"Oh yes," said Barney complacently. "Everyone knows us here."

"We shall have a lot of friends to see," said Simon rather too loudly, with a quick sideways glance at Will.

"Yes, they've been here before. They stayed for two weeks last summer," said Merriman. Barney looked at him crossly. His great-uncle's craggy, deep-lined face was impassive.

"Three weeks," said Simon.

"Was it? I beg your pardon."

"It's lovely to be back," Jane said diplomatically. "Thank you very much for letting us come, Mr Stanton, Mrs Stanton."

"You're very welcome." Will's uncle waved a hand in the air. "Things have worked out fine—you three and Will can all have a great time together, and leave us square old characters to ourselves."

There was a very small silence. Then Jane said brightly, without looking at her brothers, "Yes, we can."

Will said to Simon, "Why is it called Trewissick?"

"Er," said Simon, taken aback, "I really don't know. Do you know what it means, Gumerry?"

"Look it up," said his great-uncle coolly. "Research sharpens the memory."

Will said diffidently, "It's the place where they have the Greenwitch ceremony, isn't it?"

The Drews stared at him. "Greenwitch? What's that?"

"Quite right," Merriman said. He looked down at them, a twitch beginning at one side of his mouth.

"It was in some book I read about Cornwall," Will said.

"Ah," Bill Stanton said. "Will is quite an anthropologist, his father was telling me. Watch out. He's very big on ceremonies and such."

Will seemed to look rather uncomfortable. "It's just a sort of spring thing," he said. "They make a leaf image and chuck it into the sea. Sometimes they call it the Greenwitch and sometimes King Mark's Bride. Old custom."

"Oh yes. Like the carnival," Barney said dismissively. "In the summer."

"Well no, not quite." Will rubbed his ear, sounding apologetic. "I mean, that Lammas carnival, it's more a sort of tourist affair, isn't it?"

"Huh!" said Simon.

"He's right, you know," Barney said. "There were far more

visitors than locals dancing about the streets last summer. Including me." He looked at Will rather thoughtfully.

"Here we be!" cried Mrs Penhallow, materialising in the room with a tray of food almost as big as herself.

"Mrs Penhallow must know all about the Greenwitch," said Fran Stanton in her soft American voice. "Don't you, Mrs Penhallow?" It was a well-meaning remark intended to keep the peace, in a situation which seemed to her a little prickly. But it had the reverse effect. The small round Cornishwoman set down her tray abruptly on the table, and the smile dropped from her face.

"I don't hold with talk of witches," she said, politely but finally, and went out again.

"Oh my," said Aunt Fran in dismay.

Her husband chuckled. "Yankee, go home," he said.

*   *   *

"What is this Greenwitch affair really, Gumerry?" Simon said next morning.

"Will told you."

"All he knew was what he got out of some book."

"He's going to be a nuisance, I'm afraid," Barney said with distaste.

Merriman looked down at him sharply. "Never dismiss anyone's value until you know him."

Barney said, "I only meant—"

"Shut up, Barney," said Jane.

"The making of the Greenwitch," said Merriman, "is an old spring rite still celebrated here, for greeting summer and charming a good harvest of crops and fish. In a day or two, as it happens. If you will all tread a little more gently, Jane might be able to watch it."

22

"Jane?" said Barney. "Only Jane?"

"The making of the Greenwitch is very much a private village affair," Merriman said. Jane thought his voice seemed strained, but his face was so near the roof of the narrow landing as to be lost in shadow. "No visitors are normally allowed near. And of the locals, only women are allowed to be present."

"Good grief!" said Simon in disgust.

Jane said, "Surely we ought to be doing something about the grail, Gumerry? I mean after all that's why we're here. And we haven't got long."

"Patience," Merriman said. "In Trewissick, as you may recall, you never had to go looking for things to happen. They tended to happen to you."

"In that case," Barney said, "I'm going out for a bit." He held the flat book in his hand unobtrusively against his side, but his great-uncle looked down from a height like a lighthouse.

"Sketching?" he said.

"Uh-huh," said Barney reluctantly. The Drews' mother was an artist. Barney had always expressed horror at the idea of possessing the same talent, but in the last twelve months he had been disconcerted to find it creeping up on him.

"Try drawing this terrace from the other side," Merriman said. "With the boats as well."

"All right. Why?"

"Oh, I don't know," said his great-uncle vaguely. "It might come in handy. A present for someone. Perhaps even for me."

*   *   *

Crossing the quay, Barney passed a man sitting at an easel. It was a common enough sight in Trewissick, which like many of the more picturesque villages in Cornwall was much frequented by amateur painters. This particular artist had a very great deal of uncombed dark hair, and a square, hefty frame. Barney paused, and peeped over his shoulder. He blinked. On the easel was a wild abstract in crude bright colours, bearing no visible relation at all to the scene in the harbour before them; it was unexpected, compared to the neat, anaemic little water-colours that nineteen out of twenty Trewissick harbour-painters produced. The man was painting away like one demented. He said, without pausing or turning round, "Go away."

Barney lingered for a moment. There was real power in the painting, of a peculiar kind that made him oddly uneasy.

"Go away," the man said more loudly.

"I'm going," Barney said, moving one step backwards. "Why green, up in that top corner, though? Why not blue? Or a *better* kind of green?" He was distressed by a lurid zig-zag of a particularly nasty shade, a yellowy, mustard-like green which drew the eye away from the rest of the picture. The man began to make a low rumbling noise like a growling dog, and the broad shoulders stiffened. Barney fled. He said to himself rebelliously, "But that colour was *all wrong*."

On the far side of the harbour he perched himself on a low wall, with the steep sliced rock of the headland at his back. The ill-tempered painter was invisible from there, hidden behind one of the inevitable piles of fish-boxes on the quay. Barney sharpened a new pencil with his penknife and began to doodle. A sketch of a single fishing-boat went badly, but a rough outline of the whole harbour began to turn out well, and Barney switched from pencil to an old-fashioned soft-nibbed fountain pen of which he was particularly fond. He worked fast then, pleased with the drawing, absorbed in its detail, sensing the awareness—still new, this spring—that some-thing of himself was going out through his fingers. It was a

24

kind of magic. Coming up for air, he paused, and held the drawing out at arm's length.

And without a sound, a large dark-sleeved hand came from one side and seized the sketch pad. Before Barney could turn his head, he heard a noise of ripping paper. Then the pad was flung back at his feet, tumbling over itself on the ground. Footsteps ran. Barney leapt up with an indignant shout, and saw a man running away up the quayside, the page from the sketch pad flapping white against his dark clothes. It was the long-haired, bad-tempered painter he had seen on the quay.

"Hey!" Barney yelled, furious. "Come back!"

Without a glance behind, the man swung round the end of the harbour wall. He was a long way ahead, and the harbour path sloped uphill. Barney came tearing up just in time to hear a car engine snarl into life and roar away. He whirled round the corner into the road, and ran smack into someone walking up the hill.

"Uh!" grunted the stranger, as the breath was thumped out of him. Then his voice came back. "Barney!"

It was Will Stanton.

"A man," gasped Barney, staring around him. "Man in dark sweater."

"A man came running up from the harbour just ahead of you," Will said, frowning. "He jumped into a car and drove off that way." He pointed down into the village.

"That was him," Barney said. He peered resentfully at the empty road.

Will looked too, fiddling with his jacket zipper. He said with astonishing force, "Stupid of me, *stupid*, I knew there was something—just not properly awake, thinking of—" He shook his head as if tossing something away from it. "What did he do?"

"He's loopy. Mad." Barney could still scarcely speak for indignation. "I was sitting down there sketching, and he just came up from nowhere, ripped the drawing out of my book and belted off with it. What would any normal person do that for?"

"Did you know him?"

"No. Well, that is, I'd seen him, but only today. He was sitting down on the quay, painting, at an easel."

Will smiled broadly. A silly smile, Barney thought. "Sounds as though he thought your picture was better than his."

"Oh, come off it," Barney said impatiently.

"Well, what was his picture like?"

"Weird. Very peculiar."

"There you are, then."

"There I am not. It was weird, but it was good too, in a nasty sort of way."

"Goodness me," Will said, looking vacant. Barney glared at his round face with its thick brown fringe of hair, and felt more irritated than ever. He began trying to think of an excuse to get away.

"He had a dog in the car," Will said absent-mindedly.

"A dog?"

"Barking like anything. Didn't you hear it? And jumping about. It nearly jumped out when he got in. Hope it didn't chew up your drawing."

"I expect it did," Barney said coldly.

"Lovely dog," Will said, in the same vague, dreamy tone. "One of those long-legged Irish setters, a super reddish colour. No decent man would shut a dog like that up in a car."

Barney stood stock-still, looking at him. There was only one dog like that in Trewissick. He realised suddenly that directly across the road he could see a tall familiar grey house. At the same moment a gate at the side of the house swung open, and a man came out: a stout, elderly man with a short grey beard, leaning on a stick. Standing in the road, he put his fingers in his mouth and gave a sharp two-note whistle. Then he called, "Rufus? Rufus!"

Impulsively Barney ran towards him. "Captain Toms? You are Captain Toms, aren't you? Please, look, I know Rufus, I helped look after him last summer, and I think someone's stolen him. A man went off with him in a car, a dark man with long hair, an awful man." He paused. "Of course, if it was someone you know—"

The man with the beard looked carefully at Barney. "No," he said slowly, deliberately. "I don't know a gentleman of that description. But you do seem to know Rufus. And by that hair of yours I fancy you'd be maybe Merriman's youngest nephew. One of my tenants, last year, eh? The children with the sharp eyes."

"That's right." Barney beamed. "I'm Barnabas. Barney." But something puzzled him about Captain Toms' manner: it was almost as if he were carrying on some other conversation at the same time. The old man was not even looking at him; he seemed to be gazing blankly at the surface of the water, seeing nothing, lost in his own mind.

Barney suddenly remembered Will. He turned—and saw to his astonishment that Will too was standing near him staring vacantly at nothing, expressionless, as if listening. What was the matter with everybody? "This is Will Stanton," he said loudly to Captain Toms.

The bearded face did not change expression. "Yes," said Captain Toms gently. Then he shook his head, and seemed to wake up. "A dark man, you said?"

"He was a painter. Very bad-tempered. I don't know who he was or anything. But Will saw him going off with a dog who sounded just like Rufus—and just outside your door—"

"I will make enquiries," Captain Toms said reassuringly. "But come in, come in, both of you. You shall show your friend

27

the Grey House, Barnabas. I must find my key. . . I was busy in the garden. . . ." He felt in his pockets, patting at his jacket ineffectually with the arm not leaning on the stick. Then they were at the front door.

"The door's open!" Will said sharply. His voice was crisp, very different from his inane babbling of a few moments before, and Barney blinked.

Captain Toms pushed the half-open door with his stick, and stumped inside. "That's how the fellow got Rufus out. Opened the front door while I was round the back . . . I still can't find that key." He began fumbling in his pockets again.

Following him in, Barney felt something rustle at his feet; he bent, and picked up a sheet of white paper. "You didn't pick up your—" He stopped abruptly. The note was very short, and in large letters. He could not help taking it in at a glance. He held it out to the captain, but it was Will, this strange brisk Will, who took the paper, and stood staring at it with the old man, the two heads close, young and old, brown and grey.

The note was made of large black capital letters cut from a newspaper and stuck very neatly together on the sheet. It said, "IF YOU WANT YOUR DOG BACK ALIVE, KEEP AWAY FROM THE GREENWITCH."

CHAPTER THREE

UNDER THE SUNSET SKY THE SEA WAS GLASS-SMOOTH. LONG SLOW rollers from the Atlantic, rippling like muscles beneath the skin, made the only sign of the great invisible strength of the ocean in all the tranquil evening. Quietly the fishing-boats moved out, a broad fishtail wake spreading behind each one; their engines chugged softly through the still air. Jane stood at the end of Kemare Head, on the crest of a granite outfall that tumbled its rocks two hundred feet to the sea, and she watched them go. Toy boats, they seemed from there: the scatter of a fishing fleet that every week, every month, every year for endless years had been going out after the pilchard or the mackerel before dusk, and staying at the chase until dawn. Every year there were fewer of them, but still every year they went.

The sun dropped at the horizon, a fat glowing ball spreading yellow light over all the smooth sea, and the last boat crept out of Trewissick harbour, its engine thumping like a muffled heart-beat in Jane's ears. As the last spreading lines of the boat's wake washed against the harbour wall, in a final swift rush the great sun dropped below the horizon, and the light of the April evening began very slowly to die. A small wind sprang up. Jane shivered, and pulled her jacket around her; there was suddenly a coldness in the darkening air.

As if in answer to the beginning breeze, a light starred up suddenly across Trewissick Bay, on the headland opposite Kemare Head. At the same time there was a sudden warmth behind Jane's back. She swung round, and saw dark figures against tall flames, where a light had been set to the towering pile of driftwood and branches that had lain waiting to become a bonfire for this one night. Mrs Penhallow had told her that the two beacons would burn until the fishing-boats came back, flames leaping all through the night until the dawn.

Mrs Penhallow: now there was a mystery. Jane thought again of the moment that afternoon when she had been alone in the living-room, flipping through a magazine, waiting for Simon. She had heard a nervous clearing of the throat, and there in the kitchen doorway Mrs Penhallow was standing, round and rosy and unusually fidgetty.

"Ef you fancy comin' to the makin' tonight, m'dear, you'm welcome," she said abruptly.

Jane blinked at her. "The making?"

"The makin' of the Greenwitch." The lilt of Mrs Penhallow's Cornish accent seemed more marked than usual. "It do take all the night, 'tes a long business, and no outsiders allowed near, generally. But if you feel you'd like . . . you being the only female close to the Perfessor, and all . . ." She waved a hand as if to catch words. "The women did agree it's all right, and I'd be happy to take 'ee."

"Thank you very much," said Jane, puzzled but pleased. "Er . . . can Mrs Stanton come too?"

"No," Mrs Penhallow said sharply. She added more gently, as Jane's eyebrows went up, "She'm a furriner, you see. Tisn't fitting."

Up on the headland, gazing at the fire, Jane remembered the

flat finality of the words. She had accepted the pronouncement and, without even trying to explain the situation to Fran Stanton, had come out after supper to the headland with Mrs Penhallow.

Yet still she had been given no idea of what was to happen. Nobody had told her what the thing called the Greenwitch would be like, or how it would be made, or what would happen to it. She knew only that the business would occupy the whole night, and end when the fishermen came home. Jane shivered again. Night was falling, and she was not over-fond of the nights of Cornwall; they held too much of the unknown.

Black shadows ran over the rocks around her, dancing and disappearing as the flames leapt. Instinctively seeking company, Jane moved forward into the circle of bright light around the bonfire; yet this too was unnerving, for now the other figures moved to and fro at the edge of the darkness, out of sight, and she felt suddenly vulnerable. She hesitated, frightened by the tension in the air.

"Come, m'dear," said Mrs Penhallow's soft voice, beside her. "Come by here." There was a hint of urgency in her tone. Hastily she took Jane by the arm and led her aside. "Time for the makin'," she said. "You want to keep out of the way, if you can."

Then she was gone again, leaving Jane alone near a group of women busying themselves with something not yet visible. Jane found a rock and sat down, warmed by the fire; she watched. Scores of women were there, of all ages: the younger ones in jeans and sweaters, the rest in sturdy dark skirts, long as overcoats, and high heavy boots. Jane could see a big pile of stones, each the size of a man's head, and a far higher pile of green branches—hawthorn, she thought—too leafy to be intended for the fire. But she did not understand the purpose of either of these.

Then one tall woman moved out before the rest, and held

one arm high in the air. She called out something Jane could not understand, and at once the women set to working, in a curiously ordered way in small groups. Some would take up a branch, strip it of leaves and twigs, and test it for flexibility; others then would take the branch, and in some swift practised way weave it together with others into what began very slowly to emerge as a kind of frame.

After a while the frame began to show signs of becoming a great cylinder. The cleaning and bending and tying went on for a long time. Jane shifted restlessly. The leaves on some of the branches seemed to be of a different shape from the hawthorn. She was not close enough to see what they might be, and she did not intend to move. She felt she would only be safe here, half-invisible on her rock, unnoticed, watching from a little way off.

At her side suddenly she found the tall woman who had seemed the others' leader. Bright eyes looked down at her out of a thin face, framed by a scarf tied under the chin. "Jane Drew, it is," the woman said, with a Cornish accent that sounded oddly hard. "One of those who found the grail."

Jane jumped. The thought of the grail was never fully out of her mind, but she had not linked it with this strange ceremony here. The woman, however, did not mention it again.

"Watch for the Greenwitch," she said conversationally. It was like a greeting.

The sky was almost black now, with only a faint rim of the glow of daylight. The lights of the two bonfires burned brightly on the headlands. Jane said hastily, clutching at this companion-ship against the lonely dark, "What are they doing with those branches?"

"Hazel for the framework," the woman said. "Rowan for the head. Then the body is of hawthorn boughs, and hawthorn blossoms. With the stones within, for the sinking. And those who are crossed, or barren, or who would make any wish, must touch the Greenwitch then before she be put to cliff."

"Oh," Jane said.

"Watch for the Greenwitch," said the woman pleasantly again, and moved away. Over her shoulder she said, "You may make a wish too, if you like. I will call you, at the right time."

Jane was left wondering and nervous. The women were busier now, working steadily, singing in a strange kind of wordless humming; the cylinder shape grew more distinct, closer-woven, and they carried the stones and put them inside. The head began to take shape: a huge head, long, squarish, without features. When the framework was done, they began weaving into it green branches starred with white blossoms. Jane could smell the heavy sweetness of the hawthorn. Somehow it reminded her of the sea.

* * *

Hours went by. Sometimes Jane dozed, curled beside her rock; whenever she woke, the framework seemed to look exactly as it had before. The work of weaving seemed endless. Mrs Penhallow came twice with hot tea from a flask. She said anxiously, "Now if you do feel you've had enough, m'dear, you just say. Easy to take you along home."

"No," Jane said, staring at the great leafy image with its court of steady workers. She did not like the Greenwitch; it frightened her. There was something menacing in its broad squat shape. Yet it was hypnotic too; she could scarcely take her eyes off it. *It*. She had always thought of witches as being female, but she could feel no *she* quality in the Greenwitch. It was unclassifiable, like a rock or a tree.

The bonfire still burned, fed carefully with wood, its warmth was very welcome in the chill night. Jane moved away to stretch her stiff legs, and saw inland a faint greyness beginning to lighten the sky. Morning would be coming soon. A misty morning: fine drops of moisture were flicking at her face already. Against the lightening sky she could see Trewissick's standing stones, five of them, ancient skyward-pointing fingers halfway along Kemare Head. She thought: that's what Greenwitch is like. It reminds me of the standing stones.

When she turned back again towards the sea, the Greenwitch was finished. The women had drawn away from the great figure; they sat by the fire, eating sandwiches, and laughing, and drinking tea. As Jane looked at the huge image that they had made, out of leaves and branches, she could not understand their lightness. For she knew suddenly, out there in the cold dawn, that this silent image somehow held within it more power than she had ever sensed before in any creature or thing. Thunder and storms and earthquakes were there, and all the force of the earth and sea. It was outside Time, boundless, ageless, beyond any line drawn between good and evil. Jane stared at it, horrified, and from its sightless head the Greenwitch stared back. It would not move, or seem to come alive, she knew that. Her horror came not from fear, but from the awareness she suddenly felt from the image of an appalling, endless loneliness. Great power was held only in great isolation. Looking at the Greenwitch, she felt a terrible awe, and a kind of pity as well.

But the awe, from her amazement at so inconceivable a force, was stronger than anything else.

"You feel it, then." The leader of the women was beside her again; the hard, flat words were not a question. "A few women do. Or girls. Very few. None of those there, not one." She gestured contemptuously at the cheerful group beyond. "But one who has held the grail in her hands may feel many things. . . . Come. Make your wish."

34

"Oh no." Jane shrank back instinctively.

In the same moment a cluster of four young women broke away from the crowd and ran to the broad, shadowy leaf-image. They were shaking with giggles, calling to one another; one, larger and noisier than the rest, rushed up and clasped the hawthorn sides that stretched far above her head.

"Send us all rich husbands, Greenwitch, pray thi'!" she shouted.

"Or else send her young Jim Tregoney!" bellowed another. Shrieking with laughter, they all ran back to the group.

"See there!" said the woman. "No harm comes to the foolish, which is most of them. And therefore none to those with understanding. Will you come?"

She walked over to the big silent figure, laid a hand on it, and said something that Jane could not hear.

Nervously Jane followed. As she came close to the Greenwitch she felt again the unimaginable force it seemed to represent, but again the great loneliness too. Melancholy seemed to hover about it like a mist. She put out her hand to grasp a hawthorn bough, and paused. "Oh dear," she said impulsively, "I wish you could be happy."

She thought, as she said it: how babyish, when you could have wished for anything, even getting the grail back . . . even if it's all a lot of rubbish, you could at least have tried. . . . But the hard-eyed Cornishwoman was looking at her with an odd surprised kind of approval.

"A perilous wish!" she said. "For where one may be made happy by harmless things, another may find happiness only in hurting. But good may come of it."

Jane could think of nothing to say. She felt suddenly extremely silly.

Then she thought she heard a muffled throbbing sound out at sea; she swung round. The woman too was looking outward, at a grey streak of horizon where none had been before. Out on the dark sea, lights were flickering, white and red and green. The first fishermen were coming home.

Afterwards, Jane remembered little of that long waiting time. The air was cold. Slowly, slowly, the fishing-boats came closer, over the stone-grey sea glimmering in the cold dawn. And then, when at last they neared the wharf, the village seemed to splutter into life. Lights and voices woke on the jetties; engines coughed; the air was filled with shouting and laughing and a great bustle of unloading; and over all of it the gulls wheeled and screamed, early-woken for thievery, eddying in a great white cloud round the boats to dive for discarded fish. Afterwards, Jane found herself remembering the gulls most of all.

Up from the harbour, when the unloading was done, and lorries gone to market and boxes gone into the little canning factory—up from the harbour came a procession of the fishermen. There were others too, factory men and mechanics and shopkeepers and farmers, all the men of Trewissick, but the dark-jerseyed fishermen, shadow-eyed, bristle-chinned, weary, smelling of fish, led the long crowd. They came along the headland, calling cheerfully to the women; no meeting could have been less romantic, Jane thought, up there in the sleepless cold under the dead grey light of the dawn, and yet there was a great light-heartedness among them all. The bonfire still burned, a last stock of wood newly blazing; the men gathered round it, rubbing their hands, in a tumult of deep voices that sounded harsh in Jane's ears after the lighter chattering of the women all night.

High and low in the sky the gulls drifted, uncertain, hopeful. Amongst all the bustle stood the Greenwitch, vast and silent, a little diminished by light and noise but still brooding, ominous. Despite all the raucous exchanges tossed between the men and women there was a curious respectfulness towards the strange leafy image; a clear reluctance to make any fun of the Greenwitch. Jane found that for some reason this left her feeling relieved.

She caught sight of Merriman's tall figure at the edge of the crowd of Cornishmen, but made no attempt to reach him. This was a time simply to wait and see what might happen next. The men seemed to be gathering in one group, the women moving away. All at once Mrs Penhallow was at Jane's side again.

"Come, let me show 'ee where to go, m'dear. Now, as the sun comes up, the men do put the Greenwitch to cliff." She smiled at Jane, half earnest, half offering a self-conscious apology. "For luck, you see, and for good fishing and a good harvest. So they say. . . . But we must keep our distance, to give them a clear run." She beckoned, and Jane followed her away from the Greenwitch to the side of the headland. She had only half an idea what this was all about.

The men began to crowd round the Greenwitch. Some touched it ostentatiously, laughing, calling aloud a wish. For the first time, in the growing daylight, Jane noticed that the square, leaf-woven figure had been built on a kind of platform, like a huge tray made of boards, and that this platform had a heavy wheel at each corner, carefully wedged with big stones. Calling and whooping, the men pulled the stones from the wheels, and Jane saw the figure sway as the platform moved free. Greenwitch was perhaps half again as high as a man, but very broad for its height, with its huge square head almost as wide as its body. It did not look like a copy of a human being. It looked, Jane thought, like a single representative of a fearful unknown species, from another planet, or from some unthinkably distant part of our own past.

"Heave, boys!" a voice called. The men had attached ropes to all four sides of the platform; they milled round, holding, steadying, gently pulling the swaying image towards the end of the headland. Greenwitch lumbered forward. Jane could smell the heavy scent of the hawthorn. The blossoms seemed brighter, the green boughs of Greenwitch's sides almost luminous; she realised that inland, over the moors beyond Trewissick, the sun was coming up. Yellow light blazed out over them; a cheer rose from the crowd, and the platform with the green figure moved almost to the clutter of rocks at the edge of the cliff.

Suddenly a shout, high-pitched as a scream, rang out over the crowd; Jane jumped, and turned to see a scuffle of jostling bodies at the edge of the crowd. A man seemed to be trying to break through; she glimpsed a dark-haired head, the face twisted with fury, and then the group closed again.

"Another of they newspaper photographers, I shouldn't wonder," Mrs Penhallow said with a hint of smugness in her pleasant voice. " 'Tisn't allowed to take pictures of the Green-witch, but there's always one or two do try. The younger lads usually take care o' them."

Jane thought the younger lads were probably taking good care of this year's intruder, judging by the speed with which his threshing form was being hustled away. She looked again for Merriman, but he seemed to have disappeared. And a change in the voice of the crowd drew her eyes back to the end of Kemare Head.

A voice called again, this time with familiar words of child-hood. "One to be ready . . . two to be steady . . . three to be *off!*" Only the ropes at the rear and sides of the trolley were held now, Jane saw, by perhaps a dozen men each. At the last word of command the crowd buzzed and murmured, the lines of men ran forwards and sideways, Greenwitch lurching faster and faster before them; and then in one swift complex movement the trolley was jerked outwards over the edge of the cliff, and brought up short from falling by its ropes.

And the great green tree-woven figure of the Greenwitch, with no rope to hold it back, was flung out into the air and down over the end of Kemare Head. For a split second it was there, visible, falling, in the blue and the green among the wheeling screaming white gulls, and then it was gone, plunging down, driven by the weight of the stones inside its body. There was a silence as if all Cornwall held its breath, and then they heard the splash.

Cheers and shouts rose from the headland. People rushed to the edge of the cliff, where the rope-holders were slowly dragging the wheeled trolley back up over the rock. After a swift glance over the edge, they surrounded the heaving string of men, cheering them back along Kemare Head. When the crowd near the rocks had thinned away Jane clambered to the edge, and peered cautiously down.

Down there, the sea washed its great slow swells against the foot of the cliff as if nothing had happened. Only a few scattered twigs of hawthorn floated on the water, rising and falling with the swells, drifting to and fro.

Suddenly giddy, Jane drew back from the rocks to the edge of the cheerful Trewissick crowd. There was no smell of hawthorn now, only a mixture of wood-smoke and fish. The bonfire had burned out, and people were beginning to drift away, back to the village.

Jane saw Will Stanton before he saw her. Beside her, a group of fishermen moved away and there was Will, outlined against the grey morning sky, straight brown hair flopping down to his eyebrows, chin jutting in a way that for a split second reminded her oddly of Merriman. The boy from Buckinghamshire was gazing out to sea, unmoving, lost in some fierce private contemplation. Then he turned his head and looked straight at her.

The fierceness became a polite relaxed smile with such speed that Jane felt it was unnatural. She thought: we've been so chilly to him, he can't really be as pleased to see me as all that.

Will came towards her. "Hallo," he said. "Were you here all night? Was it exciting?"

"It went on a long time," Jane said. "The exciting part was sort of spread out. And the Greenwitch—" She stopped.

"What was the making of it like?"

"Oh. Beautiful. Creepy. I don't know." She knew she could never describe it, in the sensible light of day. "Have you been with Simon and Barney?"

"No," Will said. His gaze slid past her. "They were—busy—somewhere. With your great-uncle, I expect."

"I expect they were dodging you," Jane said, astounded at her own honesty. "They can't help it, you know. I don't think it'll last long, once they've got used to you. There's something else bothering them, you see, nothing connected with you. . . ."

"Don't worry about it," Will said. For an instant Jane was looking at a quick reassuring grin; then his eyes flicked away again. She had an embarrassing feeling that she was wasting her breath; that the Drews' rudeness had not troubled Will Stanton in the least. Hastily she took refuge in prattle.

"It was nice when the fishermen and everyone came up from the harbour. And sea gulls everywhere . . . and I saw Gumerry too, but he seems to have gone again now. Did you see him?"

Will shook his head, pushing his hands deep into the pockets of his battered leather jacket. "We're lucky he got us the chance to come up here. They're supposed to go to a lot of trouble keeping visitors out, normally."

Jane said, remembering: "There was one newspaper photographer who tried to get up close to the Greenwitch when they were taking it to the edge of the cliff. A lot of boys dragged him off. He was yelling like anything."

"A dark man? With long hair?"

"Well yes, as a matter of fact. At least I think so." She stared at him.

"Ah," Will said. His amiable round face was vacant again. "Was that before you saw Merriman, or afterwards?"

"After," Jane said, puzzled.

"Ah," Will said again.

"Hey, Jane!" Barney came skidding up, out of breath, oversize boots flapping, with Simon close behind him. "Guess what we did, we saw Mr Penhallow and he let us go on board the *White Heather*, and we helped them unload—"

"Poof!" Jane backed away. "You certainly did!" Wrinkling her nose at their scale-spattered sweaters, she turned back to Will.

But Will was not there. Gazing round, she could see no sign of him anywhere.

"Where's he gone?" she said.

Simon said, "Where's who gone?"

"Will Stanton was here. But he's vanished. Didn't you see him?"

"We must have frightened him away."

"We really ought to be nicer to him, you know," Barney said.

"Well, well, well," Simon said indulgently. "We'll keep him happy. Take him for a climb, or something. Come on, Jane, tell us about the Greenwitch."

But Jane was not listening. "That was odd," she said slowly. "I don't mean Will going off, I mean something he said. He's only known Gumerry for three days, and he's a polite sort of boy. But when he was talking about him just now, without thinking, the way things slip out naturally because you aren't watching—he didn't call Gumerry 'your great-uncle' or 'Professor Lyon,' the way he usually does. He called him 'Merriman.' Just as if they were both the same age."

CHAPTER FOUR

IT WAS THE SKY THAT BEGAN THE ODDNESS OF THE REST OF THAT day. As the Drews walked back along Kemare Head to the harbour the sun rose higher ahead of them, but gave no warmth, for as it rose a fine hazy mist began to grow too. In a little while the mist covered all the sky, so that the sun hung there familiar and yet strange, like a furry orange.

"Heat haze," said Simon when Jane pointed this out to him. "It's going to be a nice day."

"I don't know," said Jane doubtfully. "It looks funny to me, more like a kind of danger signal. . . ."

By the time they had finished their large breakfast at the cottage, served by a sleepy Mrs Penhallow, the haze was thicker.

"It'll burn off," Simon said. "When the sun gets higher."

"I wish Great-Uncle Merry would come home," said Jane.

"Stop worrying. Will Stanton isn't back yet either, they could be talking to Mr Penhallow, or someone. What's the matter with you this morning?"

"Needs a nap," Barney said. "Poor child. Had no sleep."

"Poor child, indeed," said Jane, and was overtaken by a huge yawn.

"See?" said Barney.

"Perhaps you're right," Jane said meekly, and she went to her room, setting the alarm clock to waken her in an hour's time.

When the shrilling bell buzzed through her head, it woke her into total confusion. Though the curtains were open, the room was almost dark. For a moment Jane thought it was night, and she waking early, until into her mind swam the image of the Greenwitch falling, falling down to the early-morning sea, and in alarm she jumped out of bed. The sky outside was solid with heavy dark clouds; she had never seen anything quite like it. The light was so dim that it was as if the sun had never risen that day.

Simon and Barney were alone downstairs, gazing anxiously out at the sky. Mr and Mrs Stanton, Jane knew, had left Trewissick early that morning for a two-day tour of china-clay pits; Mrs Penhallow, the boys reported, had retreated to bed. And Merriman and Will had still not appeared at all.

"But what could Gumerry be doing? Something must have happened!"

"I don't know quite what we can do, except wait." Simon was subdued now too. "I mean, we could go out to look for him, but where would we start?"

"The Grey House," Barney said suddenly.

"Good idea. Come on, Jane."

*   *   *

"He seems to be taking the appearance of a painter," Will said to Merriman as they made their way back along Kemare Head, behind the last straggle of cheerful villagers. "A swarthy kind of man, of middle height, with long dark hair and apparently a real but rather nasty talent. A nice touch, that."

"The nastiness may be unintentional," Merriman said grimly. "Even the great lords of the Dark cannot keep their true nature from colouring their dissimulations."

"You think he is one of the great lords?"

"No. No, almost certainly not. But go over the rest of it."

"He has already made a contact with the children. With Barney. And he has a totem—he stole a drawing that Barney had done, of the harbour."

Merriman hissed between his teeth. "I had a purpose for that drawing. Our friend is further ahead of us than I gave him credit for. Never underestimate the Dark, Will. I have been on the verge of it this time."

"He has also," said Will, "stolen Captain Toms' dog Rufus. He left a note warning that the dog would die if the captain went near the Greenwitch—taking care Barney would see the note too. A very neat piece of blackmail. If Captain Toms had gone up to Kemare Head after that, Barney would have thought him a murderer. . . . Of course the Dark knew he would be keeping only one of the Old Ones away from the making, but it could have helped him a lot. . . . Rufus really is a marvellous animal, though, isn't he?" For a moment Will's voice was that not of an ageless Old One but of an enthusiastic small boy.

The concern in Merriman's bleak, craggy face relaxed into a small smile. "Rufus played a part of his own in the winning of the grail last summer. He has more talent for communicating with ordinary human beings than most four-legged creatures."

At the end of the grassy headland, most of the villagers turned downhill to the quayside and the main village road. Merriman led Will straight ahead, to the higher road overlooking the harbour. Pausing to let a few other weary Greenwitch-makers pass, they crossed to the narrow grey-painted house that stood tallest of any in the terraced row. Merriman opened the front door, and they went in.

A long hallway stretched before them, hazy in the early-morning light. From an open door on their right Captain Toms said: "In here."

It was a broad room of bookshelves, armchairs, pictures of sailing-ships; he sat in a leather armchair with his right leg outstretched. Its foot, wearing a carpet slipper over a bandage, was propped on a leather-padded footstool. "Gout," said Captain Toms apologetically to Will. "Kicks up now and again, you know. Sign of a misspent youth, they say. It immobilises me just as effectively as any gentleman of the Dark could do— if our friend had had any foresight, he needn't have bothered to grab poor Rufus."

"That is a gift he lacks, I think." Merriman spread-eagled himself on a long sofa, with a small sigh of relief. "I am not quite sure why, since he is clearly of some rank. Something he dares not exercise, perhaps? Anyway the theft of the grail, the attention paid to linking up with the children, and especially Barney—they all add up in the same direction."

Captain Toms ran a finger reflectively over his close grey beard. "You think he plans to have the boy look into the grail, to find him the future. . . . the old scrying? . . . Well, it's possible."

Will said: "But is that what he wants *first?*"

"Whether it is or not, Barney will need careful watching."

"I shall haunt him," Will said. "He'll hate it." He prowled restlessly round the room, staring at pictures without seeing them. "But where is the Dark? Where is he? Not far away, I think."

"I have had that feeling too," Captain Toms said quietly from his armchair. "He is quite close by. Just after sunrise this morning I felt him go past the house, quite quickly, and there has been a faint sense of his nearness ever since."

"That was when he tried to get to the Greenwitch, before the throwing," Merriman said. "Lucky for us he failed, or the creature might have responded. The fishermen hustled him off this way—they were most indignant, and rather rough. . . . I followed into the village, until they released him. Then he put a shadow round himself, and I lost the way. But yes, he is near. One senses the ill-will."

Will stopped his prowling abruptly, stiffening like a pointing dog. Hastily Merriman swung his long legs off the sofa and stood up. "What is it?"

"Do you feel anything? Hear anything?"

"I did, I think. You're right." Captain Toms hobbled to the door, leaning heavily on his stick. "Come outside, quick."

The sound of barking rose even while they crossed the hall, and as they stood together on the steps of the Grey House it grew louder, nearer, the straining hysterical noise of a dog demanding freedom. Overhead the sky was leaden grey, and the daylight had become grim and murky. Along the road from the village, further down the hill where the harbour and the jetties began, a red flurry of speed came hurtling towards them, with the dark figure of a man running after it.

Will said sharply, on a high note of alarm: "But look—the children!"

On the quayside along the edge of the harbour road they saw Simon, Jane and Barney breaking into a run, excited, not yet seeing Rufus but responding eagerly to the sound of his bark. "Rufus!" Barney was shouting gleefully. "Rufus!"

The Old Ones stood poised, waiting.

As Rufus rushed joyfully round the corner towards the children, they saw the dark man raise his hand. In mid-air the dog froze, motionless, and dropped like a log of wood right in the children's path. Simon, thrown off balance too late to veer aside, tripped helplessly over him and fell hard to the ground. He lay still. Jane and Barney skidded to a halt, aghast.

The dark-haired man neared them, paused, raised a hand pointing at Barney—

Only Simon saw. Lying on the ground, facing the hill, drifting back out of the moment of black unconsciousness that had swallowed him when he hit the ground, he blinked his dazed eyes open. And he saw, or thought he saw, three shining figures in a great blaze of white light. They towered and grew, their brilliance blinding Simon's eyes; they seemed to be swelling towards him, and he closed his eyes against the pain of the light. His head was full of whirling noise still, he was not properly out of unconsciousness. Afterwards he was able to tell himself that it was all imagination: confusion after a blow. But the overwhelming sense of awe that had swept over him never afterwards quite left his memory.

And Jane and Barney, caught out of movement, staring horrified at the dark-haired man almost upon them now, saw only the dreadful change on his face as suddenly he reeled back, spun away from them, beneath the impact of some unseen force. Snarling with malignant fury, he seemed to be fighting a tremendous battle with—nothing. His body was rigid; the fighting was all in his eyes and the cold line of his mouth. There was a long horrible moment of waiting, as the dark figure froze, fiercely twisted under the grey light of the dark sky. Then something in him seemed to snap, and he flung round without another glance at them; rushed away and was gone.

Rufus moved, whining; Simon stirred and sat up. He got to his hands and knees over the dog, and patted his head groggily. Rufus licked his hand, struggling to his four wobbly feet like a newborn calf.

"I feel like that too," said Simon. Carefully, he stood up.

Jane prodded him with a nervous finger. "Are you all right?"

"Not a scratch."

"What happened?"

"I don't know. There was such a bright light. . . ." His voice trailed away, as he tried to remember.

"That was from banging your head," said Barney. "The man, you didn't see him, he was right on top of us and then—I don't know, something stopped him. It was weird."

"As if he had some kind of fit," said Jane. "He sort of writhed about, with this awful look on his face, and then he just dashed off."

"He was the painter. The one who took my drawing."

"Was he really? Of course, he stole Rufus too, that was why—"

But Barney was not listening. He stood gazing up at the high-sloping road beside the harbour. "Look," he said in a strange flat voice.

They looked with him, and striding down towards them from the direction of the Grey House came Merriman. His jacket flapped open, his hands were in his pockets, his wild white hair lifted in the breeze that was beginning to stir all around. He said when he reached them, "You're going to get wet if you stand about waiting for the rain."

Jane glanced up distractedly at the darkening sky. "Didn't you see what happened, just this minute?"

"Some of it," Merriman said. "Are you hurt at all, Simon?"

"I'm fine."

Barney was still gazing at him with a bemused look on his face. "It was you, wasn't it?" he said softly. "You stopped him, somehow. He's from the Dark."

"Come now, Barney," Merriman said briskly. "That's a large assumption. Let us not conjecture where your unpleasant friend came from—just enjoy the fact that he is gone, and Rufus safe and sound back again."

The red dog licked his hand, feathery tail waving furiously. Merriman rubbed his soft ears. "Go home," he said. Without a glance round, Rufus made off up the hill beside the harbour, and they watched in silence as he disappeared into the side entrance of the Grey House.

Barney said, "That's all very well, but I thought you brought us here to help?"

"Barney!" said Jane.

"You are already helping," Merriman said gently. "I told you, be patient."

Simon said, "We came out to look for you. We thought something might have happened."

"I was just in the Grey House, chatting with Captain Toms."

"Will Stanton hasn't come home since the Greenwitch thing, either."

"Just sight-seeing, I dare say. I expect we shall find him at home when we go back." Merriman glanced up again at the lowering grey clouds. A long low rumbling came from the sky over the sea. "Come along," he said. "Home. Before the storm breaks."

Jane said absently, as they trotted obediently to keep up with his long loping strides, "The poor Greenwitch, all alone there in the sea. I hope the waves don't smash it all to bits."

They scrambled up the last narrow steps to the cottage; as they reached the door, white light ripped open the sky, and a huge thumping crash echoed and re-echoed all around the bay.

Merriman said, through the noise, "I don't think they will."

*   *   *

Jane stood again on Kemare Head, but now she was alone, and the storm at its height. It seemed neither night nor day. The sky was grey all around, heavy, hanging; sharp lightning split it, thunder rumbled and thudded, echoing back from the inland moors. Gulls whirled and screamed in the wind. Below, the sea boiled, waves raging, tearing at the rocks. Jane felt herself lean on the wind, lean out over the cliff—and then leap high in the air, out, down, falling through the wind with the gulls swooping round her as she fell.

There was sick horror in the falling, but a kind of wild delight too. The great waves swirled to meet her, and with no shock nor splash nor sense of another element she was still falling, falling slowly, floating down through the green underwater where none of the wild frenzy from the storm above could reach. There was no movement but a slow swaying of weed, from the deepest touch of the great ocean swells. And before her, she saw the Greenwitch.

The great leafy image rested upright against a group of craggy rocks; they gave it shelter. The Greenwitch stood undamaged, just as Jane had seen it before, the square unhuman head set on the gigantic broad body. Its leaves and hawthorn blossoms were spread like weed in the gentle tug of the water, rippling to and fro. Small fish darted round the head. The whole structure swayed now and then, rhythmically, when the long reach of the storm-swell pulled at it.

Then as Jane watched, the swaying grew more pronounced, as though the storm were reaching deeper into the sea. She could feel the pull of the waves herself; she moved like a fish, both obeying and resisting them. Greenwitch began to turn and sway, faster, further, drawn so far in each direction that it seemed the whole figure must topple and be carried away. Jane felt a dark chill in the water, a sense of great threatening power, and to her horror the movement of the Greenwitch changed. Limbs stirred of themselves, the leafy head rippled and stirred as if it were a face. Then the coldness suddenly was gone, the sea was muted blue and green again with the weed and the fish swaying in the swell—but now the Greenwitch, she knew, was alive. It was neither good nor evil, it was simply alive, aware of her as she had all along been aware of it.

The huge leafy head turned towards her, and without a voice the Greenwitch spoke, spoke into her mind.

"I have a secret," the Greenwitch said.

Jane felt the loneliness that she had felt in the thing up on the headland, in the beginning: the sorrow and emptiness. But through it she felt the Greenwitch clutching at something for comfort, like a child with a toy—though this child was hundreds of years old, and through all its endlessly renewed life had never had such comfort before.

"I have a secret. I have a secret."

"You are lucky," Jane said.

The living tower of branches bent towards her, nearer. "I have a secret, it is mine. Mine, mine. But I will show you. If you promise not to tell, not to tell."

"I promise," Jane said.

The Greenwitch lurched sideways, all its twigs and leafy armlets rippling together in the water, and as it moved away from the shallow niche in the rocks against which it had been leaning, Jane saw something there in the shadows. It was a small bright shining thing, lying within the cleft in the rock, on the white sand; it was like a small glowing stick. It looked like nothing of importance, except that it glowed with this strange light.

As to a small child showing its toy, she said to the Greenwitch: "It's lovely."

"My secret," said the Greenwitch. "I guard it. No-one shall touch it. I guard it well, for always."

Without warning, the darkness and the chill came again over the water, infusing the whole undersea world. The Greenwitch changed utterly, in an instant. It became hostile, angry, threatening. It loomed over Jane.

"You'll tell! You'll tell!"

The leafy head split horribly into a parody of a face, snarling,

51

furious; the branching form seemed to spread, opening, grasping out to envelop her as the Greenwitch lurched inexorably forward. Jane backed away in terror, cowering down. The water was very hot suddenly, fierce, oppressive, full of roaring noise.

"I won't tell! I promise! I promise! *I promise. . . .*"

Cold air was on her face. "Jane! Wake up! Come on, Jane, wake up now, it's all over, it's not real . . . Jane, wake up. . . ." Merriman's deep voice was soft but insistent, his hands strong and reassuring on her shoulders. Jane sat bolt upright in the little bedroom, looked at his face, leant her damp forehead on his arm and burst into tears.

"Tell me about it," said Merriman soothingly.

"I can't! I promised!" The tears came faster.

"Now look here," Merriman said when she was calmer. "You had a bad nightmare, and it's all over. I heard a very muffled sort of shout in here and when I came in you were right down among the bedclothes, must have been as hot as blazes. No wonder you dreamed. Now tell me about it."

"Oh dear," said Jane miserably. She told him.

"Mmm," said Merriman, when she had finished. His bleak, bony face was in shadow; she could read nothing from it.

"It was awful," Jane said. "The last bit."

"I'm sure it was. Last night's doings were too rich a diet for your imagination, I'm afraid."

Jane managed a small weak grin. "We had apple pie and cheese for supper tonight. That might have helped too."

Merriman chuckled and stood up, looming against the low ceiling. "All right now?"

"All right. Thank you." As he went out she said, "Gumerry?"

"What is it?"

"I really do feel sorry for the Greenwitch, still."

"I hope you may retain that emotion," said Merriman obscurely. "Sleep well now."

Jane lay tranquil, listening to the rain against the window, and the last rumbles of the dying storm. Just before she drowsed away she thought, in a sudden flash of remembering, that she recognised the small bright object that in her dream had been the Greenwitch's secret. But before she could catch at the memory, she was asleep.

CHAPTER FIVE

SIMON BURROWED DEEPER INTO THE SMALL COSY CAVE BETWEEN pillow and bedclothes. "Mmmmmff. Nya. Go away."

"Oh come on, Simon." Barney tugged persistently at the sheet. "Get up. It's a super morning, come and see. Everything's all shiny from the rain last night, we could go down to the harbour before breakfast. Just for a walk. No-one else is awake. Come on."

Growling, Simon opened one eye and blinked at the window. In the clear blue sky a sea gull turned and lazily drifted, arching down on unmoving wings. "Oh well," he said. "All right."

In the harbour, nothing moved. Boats hung motionless at their moorings, their mast-images unrippled in the still water. There was a sea-smell of creosote from nets draped for mending over the harbour wall. Nothing broke the silence but the clatter of a distant milk-van somewhere high up in the village. The boys pattered down rain-patched steps and through narrow alleys, down to the sea. The sunshine on their faces was already warm.

As they stood looking down at the nearest boats a village mongrel trotted up, sniffed amiably at their heels, and went on his way.

54

"Rufus might be out too," Barney said. "Let's go and see."

"All right." Simon ambled after him, content, relaxed in the stillness and the sunshine and the gentle swish of the sea.

"There he is!" The rangy red dog came bounding towards them across the quayside. He pranced about them, tail waving, white teeth grinning as the long pink tongue lolled out.

"Idiot dog," said Simon affectionately as the tongue curled wetly round his hand.

Barney squatted down and gazed solemnly into Rufus's brown eyes. "I do wish he could talk. What would you tell us, boy, eh? About the painter from the Dark, and where he took you? Where was it, Rufus? Where did he hide you, eh?"

The setter stood still for a moment, looking at Barney; then he cocked his narrow head on one side and gave a curious noise that was half-bark, half-whine, like a kind of question. He swung round, lollopped a few paces along the quay, then stopped and looked back at them. Barney stood up slowly. Rufus trotted away a few more steps, then again turned and looked back, waiting for them.

"What on earth?" said Simon, watching.

"He wants to show us!" Barney hopped nervously up and down. "Come on, Simon, quick! He'll show us where the painter hides, I bet you, and we shall be able to tell Gumerry!"

Rufus whined, questioning.

"I don't know," Simon said. "We ought to get home. Nobody knows where we are."

"Oh come on, quick, before he changes his mind." Barney grabbed his arm and tugged him after the lean red dog, already trotting away now confidently across the quay.

Rufus led them straight across the harbour and round into the road that ran inland from the Grey House and the sea; the road was familiar at first, leading back through the narrowest

55

part of the village, past quiet cottages sleeping behind lace-curtained windows, and once or twice a modest house grandly labelled PRIVATE HOTEL. Then they were behind Trewissick, in the hedge-rimmed farmland that curved around the white cones and green ponds of the clay-burrow country, until, far inland, it met the moors.

Simon said, "We can't go much farther, Barney. We shall have to turn back."

"Just a little bit more."

On they went, along silent roads bright with the springtime green of newly full trees. Simon looked around him, with the flickerings of unease in his mind. Nothing was wrong: the sun warmed them; dandelions brightly starred the grass; what could be wrong? Suddenly Rufus turned off the road into a narrow, leafy lane; a signpost at the corner read PENTREATH FARM. On either side, the trees reached their branches up and over to arch in a leafy roof; even in full daylight the lane was shadowed, cool, with only a faint dappling of sunshine filtering through the leaves. All at once Simon was filled with an immense foreboding. He stood stone-still.

Barney looked over his shoulder. "What's wrong?"

"I don't know, exactly."

"Did you hear something?"

"No. I just . . . it's as if I've been here before. . . ." Simon shivered. "It's the funniest feeling," he said.

Barney looked at him nervously. "P'raps we really should go back?"

Simon did not answer; he was staring ahead, frowning. Rufus, who had disappeared round a corner in the lane for a moment, was bounding back again in a great unexplained hurry.

"Into the trees, quick!" Simon grabbed Barney's arm, and with the dog close behind them they slipped into the thicket of trees and brush that edged each side of the road. In there, picking their way carefully from tree to tree to avoid rustling footfalls, they inched forward until they could see the part of the lane that lay ahead, round the corner. They did not speak or whisper; they scarcely breathed, and at their feet Rufus crouched still as a dead dog.

There ahead, the trees were no longer thick, the land no longer a leafy tunnel. Instead they saw a wide field scattered with large single trees and clumps of scrub. Across it, the lane was no more than a grassy track, two wheel-worn ruts, winding away to where the trees grew thick again. It did not look as though many people used the path to Pentreath Farm. And there was no sign of any farmhouse. Instead, clear ahead of them in the sunlit field, they saw a caravan.

It stood tall and glittering and handsome: a real old-fashioned Gipsy caravan, of a kind they had never seen before except in pictures. Above the high wood-spoked wheels rose white wooden sides, sloping gently outwards, up to the curved wooden roof with its cone-hatted chimney. At each corner between roof and walls, brightly-painted scrollwork filled the eaves. In the side walls, square windows were set, neatly curtained; leaning down from the front of the van were shafts for the horse that stood grazing quietly nearby. At the rear, a sturdy six-rung ladder led up to a door painted with ornate decorations to match the scrollwork: a split door, of the kind used in stables, with the top half hanging open and the lower half latched shut.

As they crouched behind the trees, breathlessly staring, a figure appeared in the doorway, opened this lower door and began descending the steps of the caravan. Barney tightened his grip on Simon's arm. There was no mistaking the long wild dark hair, the snarling brow; the painter was even dressed exactly as he had been both times before, like a fisherman, in navy-blue jersey and trousers. He swallowed nervously at the impact of the man's nearness; it was as if there were a cloud of malevolence all around him. Barney was suddenly very glad that they were deep in the trees, out of all possible sight. He stood very still indeed, praying that Rufus would not make a sound.

But although indeed there was no sound anywhere in the clearing, except the clear morning song of birds in the trees, the dark man paused suddenly at the bottom of the caravan steps. He lifted his head and turned it all round, like a deer questing; Barney saw that his eyes were shut. Then the man turned full in their direction, the cold eyes opened beneath the lowering brows, and he said clearly, "Barnabas Drew. Simon Drew. Come out."

No thought of running away came into their minds, or anything but unquestioning obedience. Barney walked automatically forward out of the trees, and felt Simon moving with him in the same unhesitating way. Even Rufus trotted docile at their side.

They stood together in the sunlit field beside the caravan, facing the dark man in his dark clothes, and although the sun was warm on their skin it seemed to them that the day had become chill. The man looked at them, unsmiling, expressionless. "What do you want?" he said.

Somewhere in Barney's mind, as a spark flickers and finds tinder and blazes up into a flame, a small light of resentment flared suddenly into a crossness that burned away fear. He said boldly, "Well, for one thing I'd like my drawing back."

Beside him he half-saw Simon shake his head a little, like one pushing away sleep, and knew that he too was clear of the spell. He said more loudly, "You stole my drawing, down in the harbour, goodness knows why. And I liked it, and I want it back."

The dark eyes contemplated him coolly; it was impossible to read any emotion behind them. "Quite a promising little scribble, for your age."

"Well, you certainly don't need it," Barney said; for a moment he spoke with admiration, thinking of the real power in the man's painting.

"No," said the man, with an odd, grim half-smile. "Not now." He moved back up the steps and through the double door; over his shoulder he said, "Very well, then. Come on."

Rufus, who had stood stock-still from the beginning, began a low rumbling growl deep in his throat. Simon put a hand down to quiet him, and said, "That wouldn't be very sensible, Barney."

But Barney said lightly, "Oh no, I think it would be all right," and he moved towards the caravan steps. Simon had no choice but to follow him. "Stay, Rufus," he said. The setter folded his long legs and lay down at the foot of the steps, but still the long low growl went on eerie and unbroken; they could hear it soft in the background like a reminder of warning.

The dark man had his back to them. "Look well at the Romany vardo," he said, without turning. "There are few of them to be seen any more."

"Romany?" said Simon. "Are you a Gipsy?"

"Half Romany chal," the man said, "and half gorgio." He turned and stood with arms folded, surveying them. "I am part Gipsy, yes. That's the best you'll find these days, on the road at any rate. Even the vardo is only part Gipsy."

He nodded at the roof of the caravan, and they saw, looking up, that it was edged all about with the same brightly-painted scrollwork that decorated the outside, and that tools of some small kind hung all over one wall, with an old fiddle and an oddly-striped woollen rug. But the furniture was shiny-cheap and modern, and the chimney was not a real chimney, but only a vent for carrying away hot air from above the neat electric stove.

Then they saw suddenly that the ceiling was painted. From end to end, above the bright conventional curlicues of the scrollwork, a huge churning abstract painting was spread above their heads. There was no recognisable form to its shapes and colours, yet it was a disturbing, alarming sight, full of strange whorls and shadows and shot through with lurid colours that jarred on the senses. Barney felt again the power and the nastiness that had leapt at him from the canvas he had seen the man painting in the harbour; up on this ceiling too he saw the particular unnerving shade of green he had found so unpleasant out there. He said suddenly to Simon, "Let's go home."

"Not yet," said the dark man. He spoke softly, without moving, and Barney felt a chill awareness of the Dark reaching out to control him—until without warning a faint hissing sound that had been vaguely puzzling him erupted into the boiling of a kettle, and a shrill whistle filled the room and made a sense of evil suddenly ridiculous.

But Simon had felt it too. He looked at the dark man and thought: *you keep steering us away from being frightened, delaying it. Why do you want us to stay?*

The dark-haired man busied himself with the prosaic matter of spooning instant coffee into a mug and pouring on water from the kettle. "Either of you drink coffee?" he said over his shoulder.

Simon said quickly, "No thank you."

Barney said, "I wouldn't mind a drink of water." Seeing Simon's scowl, he added plaintively, "Well, I did get awfully thirsty walking. Not just a drink of water from the tap?"

"In that cupboard by your right foot," the painter said, "you will find some cans of orange soda." He moved to the small table at the end of the caravan, stirring his coffee. "Sealed," he added with a deliberate ironic stare at Simon. "Fizzy. Harmless. Straight from the factory."

"Thanks," Barney said promptly, bending to the cupboard door.

The man said, "You might bring out a cardboard box you'll find in there, too."

"All right." After some bumping and rattling, Barney came up with an unremarkable brown box; set it on the table and produced two drinks from the crook of his elbow. Without comment Simon took one, and popped open the top, to a reassuring hiss; but a stubborn caution still made him reluctant to drink, and he made only a pretence of swigging at the can. Barney drank thirstily, with appreciative gurgling noises.

"That's better. Thanks. Now may I have my picture back?"

"Open the box," the man said, the long hair falling about his face as he drank from his mug.

"Is it in there?"

"Open the box," the man said again, with a faint edge of strain in his voice. Simon thought: *he's as tense as a strung wire. Why?*

Setting down his drink on the table, Barney opened the top of the brown cardboard box. He took out a sheet of paper, and held it up critically. "Yes, that's my drawing."

He glanced back into the box, and then all at once a brightness was in his eyes, a fierce brilliance flashing into his brain, and he was staring in disbelief, crying out in a voice that broke into huskiness.

"Simon! It's the grail!"

In the same instant the world about them changed; with a crash the doors of the little caravan swung shut, and blinds fell over the windows, cutting out all light of day. There was an instant of black darkness, but almost at once Barney found himself blinking in a dim light. Wildly he looked round for its source, and then he realised with a sick shock that the glow, still dim, disturbing, came not from any lamp but from the painted ceiling. Up on the roof, the eerie green whorls that had so troubled him were shining with a cold bleak light. They had shapes, he saw now; angular shapes arranged in groups, like a kind of unknown writing. In the cold green light he looked down, fearful, disbelieving, and saw the same wonderful familiar object that he had seen before gleaming inside the cardboard box. Gently he lifted it out, forgetting everything around him, and set it on the table.

Simon breathed, beside him, "It is!"

Before them on the table the Cornish grail glowed: the little golden goblet that they had first seen, after so hard a search, deep in a cave beneath the cliffs of Kemare Head, and that they had saved from the people and the power of the Dark, for a while. They did not understand what it was, or what it could do; they knew only that to Merriman and the Light it was one of the great Things of Power, something of infinite value, and that one day it would come into its own when the strange runic signs and words engraved over its sides could be understood. Barney gazed as he had gazed a thousand times before at the pictures and patterns and incomprehensible signs on the golden sides of the grail. If only, if only . . . but the ancient lead-encased manuscript that they had found with the grail, in that deep lost cave, lay now at the bottom of the sea, flung by Barney himself from the end of Kemare Head in the last desperate effort to save grail and manuscript from the pursuing Dark. Though the grail had been saved, the manuscript had come to the sea, and only in that manuscript was the secret by which the vital message written on the grail could be understood. . . .

The dim light in the caravan could not dull the glow that came from the grail; yellow it blazed like a fire before them, warm, glittering. Simon said softly,"It's all right. Not a scratch on it."

A cold voice from the shadows said, "It is in good hands."

Abruptly they were out of their absorption with the grail and back in the ominous half-light of the painter of the Dark. The man's black-bead eyes glittered at them from behind the table; he was a surreal pattern of black and white, black eyes, white face, black hair. And there was a deeper strength and confidence in the voice now, a note of triumph.

"I allow you a sight of the grail," he said, "to make a bargain with you."

"You make a bargain with us?" Simon said, his voice coming out higher and louder than he had intended. "All you do is steal things. Barney's drawing, Captain Toms' dog. And the grail—it must have been you who stole it from the Museum, or your friends—"

"I have no friends," said the man unexpectedly, swiftly; it seemed a bitter reaction that he could not help, and for a moment there was a faltering of his cold gaze as he knew it. In the next instant he was composed again, looking down at them both in total self-possession.

"Stealing can be a means to an end, my young friend. My end is very simple, and there is no harm in it. All I require is five minutes of your time. Of your small brother's time, that is, and of a certain . . . talent . . . that he has."

"I'm not leaving him alone, not for a minute," Simon said.

"I did not suggest you should."

"What, then?"

Barney said nothing, but watched, cautiously. For once he felt no resentment that Simon should be taking over. Deep inside his mind something was beginning to fear this strange taut white-faced man more and more, perhaps because he had so clearly blazing a talent. It would have been much easier to face an uncomplicated monster.

The painter looked at Barney. He said, "It is very simple, Barnabas Drew. I shall take the cup that you choose to call the grail, and I shall pour into it some water, and a little oil. Then I shall ask you to sit calmly, and look into the cup, and tell me what you see."

Barney stared at him in amazement. Like a sea-mist a strange idea wreathed into his mind: was the man not evil at all, but simply off his head, a little mad? That could, he suddenly realised, explain everything the strange painter had done; after all, even great artists sometimes did odd things, acted strangely; think of nutty Van Gogh. . . .

He said carefully, "Look at the water, and the oil, and tell you what I see? Oil does make nice patterns on water, and colours . . . well, that sounds harmless enough. Doesn't it, Simon?"

"I suppose so," Simon said. He was staring hard at the dark man, at the wild eyes and the pale intent face, and the same hypnotic suggestion was creeping into his own mind. He too was thinking it more and more likely that their supposed adversary might not have anything to do with the Dark at all, whatever Great-Uncle Merry may have thought, but be simply an eccentric, a harmless nut. In which case, it would be safest to humour him.

"Yes," he said firmly. "Why not?"

Simon thought: when this daftness is all over, we can grab the grail and run. Give him the slip somehow, call Rufus in, get the grail back to Gumerry. . . . He looked hard at Barney, trying to communicate; nudged him surreptitiously and flicked his eyes at the grail. Barney nodded. He knew what his brother was trying to tell him; the same thought was only too vivid in his own mind.

The dark man ran some water from the tap into a glass and poured it into the grail. Then he took a small brown bottle from a shelf near the table and added a drop or two of some kind of oil. He looked greedily at Barney. The tension in him sang like a plucked wire.

"Now," he said. "Sit down, here, and look hard. Look hard, look long. And tell me what you see."

Barney sat in the chair before the table, and slowly took the glowing golden chalice in both his hands. Though the inscribed gold of the outside was as bright as it had ever been, the inside surface was a dull black. Barney stared down at the liquid in the bowl. In the cold green light from above his head, incomprehensibly shining out from the patterns of the painted ceiling, he watched the thin, thin layer of oil on the surface of the water swirl and coil into itself, curving, breaking and joining again, forming islands that drifted out and then vanished, merging into the rest. And he saw . . . he saw. . . .

Darkness took hold of his brain like sudden sleep, and he knew nothing more.

CHAPTER SIX

JANE WAS ALMOST IN TEARS. "BUT THEY COULDN'T JUST DIS-
appear! Something awful must have happened!"

"Nonsense," Merriman said. "They'll be rushing in any
moment now, demanding their breakfasts."

"But breakfast was more than an hour ago."

Jane stared distractedly out over the harbour, busy and
bustling in the sunshine. They stood on the little paved path
outside the cottages, above the winding web of stairs and alleys
that led down to the harbourside.

Will said, "I'm sure they're all right, Jane. They must have
woken up early and wandered out for a walk, and gone farther
than they intended. Don't worry."

"I suppose you're right. I'm sure you are. It's just that I
keep having this awful picture in my mind of them going out
to Kemare Head, the way we used to, last year, and one of
them getting stuck on the cliff, or something. . . . Oh dear, I
know I'm being stupid. I'm sorry, Gumerry." Jane shook back
her long hair impatiently. "It all comes of seeing the Greenwitch falling, I suppose. I'll shut up."

"I tell you what," said Will. "Why don't we go out to Kemare
Head just to check? You'd feel a lot happier?"

Brightening, she gazed from one to the other of them. "Could we really?"

"Of course we could," Merriman said. "Mrs Penhallow will give the truants their breakfast if they arrive in the meantime. You two start off—I'll have a word with her, and catch you up."

Jane beamed. "Oh, that's much better. Waiting's awful. Thank you, Will."

"Don't mention it," said Will cheerfully. "Lovely morning for a walk."

Into Merriman's mind he said unhappily, "*The Dark has them, I think. You feel it?*"

"*But without harm,*" came the answer cool into his thoughts. "*And perhaps to our gain.*"

*   *   *

Barney stood at the door of the caravan, blinking in the sunlight. "Well," he said, "aren't we going to get them?"

"What?" Simon said.

"The drinks, of course."

"What drinks?"

"What's the matter with you? The drinks he just offered us. He said, there are cans in the little cupboard, you can help yourselves. And something about a cardboard box." Turning to go in, he glanced at his brother in amusement. He stopped abruptly.

"Simon, what *is* the matter?"

Simon's face was white and strained, the lines of it drawn downwards in a strange adult expression of concern and distress. He stared at Barney for a moment, and then he seemed to make a great effort and wrench himself on to the same level of conversation. "You get them," he said. "The drinks. You get them. Bring them out here. It's nice in the sunshine."

There was a sound behind them inside the caravan, and Barney saw Simon jump as if he had been stabbed; then again he saw the same straining for control. Simon leaned back against the wall of the caravan, his face up to the sun. "Go on," he said.

Puzzled, Barney went into the caravan, its interior bright with the sunshine streaming in through the windows. The dark painter was sipping a cup of coffee, leaning on the table.

"This one?" Barney waved a foot at the little cupboard under the sink.

"That's right," the man said.

Down on his knees, Barney took out two cans of orange soda then peered round the dark little cupboard. "You said a cardboard box, but I can't see one."

"Not important," said the painter.

"There's something, though—" Barney reached in, and took out a piece of paper. After one glance he sat back on his heels and looked up at the man without expression. "It's my drawing. That you took."

"Well," said the man. "That's what you came for, isn't it?" His dark eyes glinted coldly at Barney beneath the scowling brows. "Take it, and drink your drink, and go."

Barney said, "I'd still like to know why you ran off with it."

"You irritated me," the man said shortly. He put down his coffee cup and motioned Barney towards the door. "No brat criticises my work. Don't start again." His voice rose ominously as Barney opened his mouth. "Just go now."

Simon said from the doorway, "What's the matter?"

"Nothing," said Barney. Rolling up the drawing, he picked up the two cans and went to the door.

"I'm not really thirsty," Simon said.

"Well, I am." Barney drank deep.

The painter stood watching them, scowling, barring their way back into the caravan. Outside in the sunshine his big horse moved one placid step forward, rhythmically ripping at the grass.

Simon said, "May we go now?"

The man's eyes narrowed; he said swiftly, "I have no hold over you. Why ask me?"

Simon shrugged. "Just now Barney said, let's go home, and you said, not yet. That's all."

A kind of relief seemed to flicker over the other's dark face. "Your brother has his precious drawing, so go, go. Up to the left of the farm"—he waved a hand at the grassy lane disappearing on round the corner—"you'll find a short cut back to the village. The path's a little overgrown, but it will take you to Kemare Head."

"Thank you," Simon said.

"Good-by," said Barney.

They went on across the field, without looking back. It was like coming out of a dark mist.

"D'you think it's a trap?" Barney whispered. "Someone might be lying in wait for us at the farm."

"Too complicated," Simon said. "He doesn't need traps."

"All right." Trotting alongside, Barney peered at him curiously. "Simon, you really do look awful. Are you sure you're all right?"

"Do shut up about it," Simon said, fierce and low. "I'm fine. Just get a move on."

"Look!" said Barney in a moment as they rounded the corner. "It's empty!"

A low grey stone farmhouse faced them, obviously deserted: nothing moved anywhere, old pieces of machinery lay rusting in the yard, and several windows gaped black and jagged-edged. The thatched roof of an out-house was sagging ominously; brambles waved wild green arms where the woods were stealing in towards the house.

"No wonder he's living in a caravan. D'you think he's really half Gipsy?"

"I doubt it," Simon said. "Just a handy explanation for looking different. And for the caravan. I don't know why but Gumerry will. There's the path." He headed for a break in the tangled growth near the old house, and they pushed their way along a narrow, bramble-crossed track.

"I'm ravenous," Barney said. "Hope Mrs Penhallow's got eggs and bacon."

Simon glanced round, his face still drawn. "I've got to talk to Gumerry. We both have. I can't explain yet, but it's terribly urgent."

Barney stared. "Well, won't he be at home?"

"Might be. But they'll have had breakfast ages ago, they'll be out looking for us."

"Where?"

"I don't know. We could try the Grey House, to begin with."

"Okay," Barney said cheerfully. "This path must come out pretty near there. And we can—" He stopped dead, staring at Simon. "Rufus! We didn't bring him back! Simon, how awful, I clean forgot about him! Where did he go?"

"He ran away. That's one of the things I have to explain about." Wearily Simon went on up the path. "It's all part of the same thing. And we've just got to find Great-Uncle Merry as soon as we possibly can, or something's going to go horribly wrong."

*   *   *

"There's no sign of them up here." Will came clambering back across the rocks at the tip of Kemare Head.

"No," Merriman said. He stood still, the sea wind blowing his white hair back like a flag.

"They might have climbed down into the next bay, to the rocks at the bottom," Jane said. "Let's go and see."

"All right."

"Wait," Merriman said. As they turned in surprise he raised an arm and pointed inland, back along the headland towards the silent grey group of standing stones that overlooked Trewissick Bay. For a moment Jane noticed nothing. Then she saw a patch of brownish red moving towards them very fast, a patch that resolved itself in a few moments into the form of a desperately-running dog.

"Rufus?"

The red setter skidded to a halt in front of them, panting, trying to bark in odd little gasping coughing sounds.

"He's always rushing up from nowhere trying to tell people things," said Jane helplessly, crouching to rub his head. "If only he could talk. Want to come with us, Rufus? Want to come and help find Barney and Simon?"

But it was very soon clear that Rufus wanted nothing but to persuade them to go back along the headland the way they had come. He jumped and whined and barked, and so they followed him. And as they came closer to the standing stones, the great grey monoliths of granite in their lonely group up on the windy grass, they saw coming towards them from the village Simon, Barney and Captain Toms. They were moving slowly, the old man still hobbling with a stick; Jane could sense the suppressed impatience in the boys' deliberate pace.

Merriman stood beside the standing stones as they came up to him. He looked only at Simon, and he said, "Well?"

* * *

"So he poured a little drop of some sort of oil into the grail," Simon said, "so that it floated on top of the water, and Barney had to sit down and stare at it."

"Sit down?" Barney said. "Where?"

"At the table. In the caravan. It was all dark, except for this funny kind of green light coming from the ceiling."

"I don't remember any green light. And for goodness' sake, Simon, I'd remember if I'd seen the grail for even a second— and I know I didn't."

"*Barney,*" Simon said; his voice shook with strain, and he leant against the nearest standing stone. "Will you shut up? You were in a spell of some sort, you don't remember anything."

"Yes I do, I remember everything we did there, but there was hardly anything. I mean we were only there a minute or two, for me to get my drawing. And I never sat down inside—"

"Barnabas," Merriman said. The voice was very soft, but there was a cold fierceness in it that made Barney sit still as stone; he said in a whisper, "I'm sorry."

Simon was paying him no attention. His eyes were glazed, inturned, as if he were seeing something that was not there. "Barney looked into the grail for a while, and then the van seemed to go very cold and it was horrible all of a sudden. He started to talk, but"— he swallowed— "it . . . it wasn't his voice that came out, it was different, and the way he talked was different too, the kind of words. . . . He said a lot of things I didn't understand, about someone called Anubis, and making ready for the great gods. Then he said, '*They are here,*' though he didn't say who he meant. And the painter, the man from the Dark, he began asking questions, and Barney would answer them, but in this funny deep voice that just wasn't like his, but like someone else."

Simon shifted restlessly; they all sat round him among the great stones, listening, intent, silent. The wind sang softly in the grass, and round the towering columns. "He said, '*Who has it?*' And Barney said, '*The Greenwitch has it.*' He said, '*Where?*' and Barney said, '*In the green depths, in the realm of Tethys, out of reach.*' The painter said, '*Not out of my reach.*' Barney didn't say anything for a bit, and then he went into his own voice, you could tell he was describing something he could see. He sounded very excited, he said, '*There's this weird great creature, all green, and darkness all round it except in one place where there's a terrible bright light, too bright to look at . . . and it doesn't like you, or me, or anybody, it won't let anyone come near. . . .*' The painter was all wound up, so twitchy he could hardly sit still, he said, '*What spell will command it?*' And all of a sudden it wasn't Barney any more, his face went empty again and that other horrible deep voice came out, and it said, '*The spell of Mana and the spell of Reck and the spell of Lir, and yet none of these if Tethys has a mind against you. For the Greenwitch will be the creature of Tethys very soon now, with all the force of all life that came out of the sea.*' "

"Ah," Captain Toms said.

Will said sharply, "The spell of Mana and the spell of Reck and the spell of Lir. Are you sure that's what he said?"

Weary and resentful, Simon raised his head and looked at him with dislike. "Of course I'm sure. If you heard a voice like that coming out of your brother's mouth, you'd remember every word it said for the rest of your life."

Will nodded gently, his round face expressionless, and Merriman said impatiently, "Get on, get on."

"The painter came very close to Barney then, whispering," Simon said. "I could scarcely hear him. He said, '*Tell me if I am observed.*' I thought Barney was going to pass out. He stared into the grail, and his face got twisted and you could see the whites of his eyes, but then he was all right again and the voice out of him said, '*You are safe if you keep from using the Cold Spells.*'

And the man nodded his head and made a kind of hissing noise and looked very pleased. He leant back in his chair and I think he had asked all he wanted to, and he was going to stop. But all of a sudden Barney sat up very straight, and that horrible voice said, very loudly like shouting, '*Unless you find the secret of the Thing of Power in this high part of spring, the grail must go back to the Light. You must make haste, before the Greenwitch departs to the great deeps, you must make haste.*' Then it stopped, and Barney sort of slumped down in his chair, and"— Simon's voice wavered, and he sniffed hard, fiercely raising his head— "and I grabbed him to make sure he was all right, and the painter was furious and yelled at me. I suppose he thought I'd broken the spell or whatever. So I got cross too, and yelled back that he wouldn't get very far when we told you all about this. And he just sat back then, with a nasty sort of smile, and said that he only had to snap his fingers and we would forget everything that had happened for as far back as he chose."

"And Barney did," Jane said shakily. "But you didn't."

Simon said, "We heard Rufus barking outside the door then, so Barney and I both moved to get him, and the dark man jumped up and snapped his fingers once, click, right by our faces. I saw Barney's eyes go sort of vague, and he moved forwards very slowly and opened the door as if he were sleepwalking. So I copied whatever he did, because obviously I had to take terrific care the painter didn't suspect I could remember what had happened. Rufus had gone. Run away. Barney blinked a bit, and shook his head, and almost at once he was talking as if we had just got there a moment or two before. Like going back in time. So I tried to do the same."

"You didn't do too well," Barney said. "You looked awful, I thought you were going to be sick."

"What happened to the grail?" Jane said.

"I suppose he's still got it."

"I wouldn't know," said Barney. "I don't remember seeing it. I do remember him giving me back my drawing, though. Look." He waved it at Merriman, who took it and twirled it absently in his fingers as he watched Simon.

"Simon," Jane said. "Why did the forgetting work on Barney and not on you?"

"It was the drinks," Simon said. "This really sounds stupid, but it must have been. We drank some orange soda, and there must have been a kind of potion in it."

"Clumsy," Merriman said. "Old-fashioned. Interesting." He looked at Will, and Will looked at him, and their eyes became opaque.

"But the orange was sealed in cans," Barney said incredulously. "That's the only reason we drank it, because he couldn't have put anything in it. And anyway, you didn't even open yours."

"The spell of Mana," Will Stanton said, very low, to Merriman. "And the spell of Reck."

"And the spell of Lir."

"No, Barney," Simon said. "You actually went and got those drinks twice, only the first time was one of the things you've forgotten. And though I didn't have any the second time, I did pretend to drink some the first time. So he thought it worked on us both."

Will said to Merriman, "There is no more time. We must go now, at once."

Simon, Jane and Barney stared at him. There was crisp, unboyish decision in his voice. Merriman nodded, his hawk's face grim and taut; he said unfathomably to Captain Toms, "Take care of them." Then he turned his cold grim face to Simon and said, "You are sure that at the last, the voice that came from Barney said, 'Before the Greenwitch departs to the great deeps'?"

"Yes," said Simon nervously.

"Then it is still here," Will said, and to the children's bewilderment he and Merriman turned and ran, ran towards the end of the headland, and the sea beyond.

With swift ease of animals they ran, the long lean man and the sturdy boy, an urgent loping running that took away their age and all sense of familiarity in their appearance; faster, faster, faster. And at the rocks ending the headland they did not pause, but went on. Will leapt up light-footed to the crest of Kemare Head and cast himself outwards into the air, into empty sky, arms spread wide, lying on the wind like a bird; and after him went Merriman, his white hair flying like a heron's crest. For an instant the two dark spread-eagled figures seemed to hang in the sky, then with a slowness as if time held its breath they curved downwards, and were gone.

Jane screamed.

Simon said, choking with horror, "They'll be killed! They'll be killed!"

Captain Toms turned to them, his rosy face stern. He did not lean on his stick; he seemed taller than before. He pointed one arm straight at them with the five fingers spread wide. "Forget," he said. "Forget."

They stood poised for a moment, caught out of awareness, and compassionately he watched the terror drain out of their faces to leave them empty, expressionless.

He said gently, "The mission for all of us is to keep the man of the Dark from the Greenwitch. Will and your great-uncle have gone among the fishermen, one way—we four have another way to watch, from your cottage and the Grey House. Know this, now. Have no fear."

Slowly he lowered his arm, and like puppets the children came back to life.

"We'd better get going, then," Simon said. "Come on, Jane."

"I go with you, Captain, right?" Barney said.

"I'll give you some breakfast," Captain Toms said, twinkling at him, leaning on his cane. "It's past time."

CHAPTER SEVEN

LIKE DIVING BIRDS THEY FLASHED INTO THE WATER, LEAVING NO ripple in the great Atlantic swells. Down through the green waves, the dim green light; though they breathed as fishes breathe, yet they flickered through the water like bars of light, with a speed no fish could ever attain.

Miles away and fathoms deep they sped, on and on, towards the distant deeps. The sea was full of noises, hissing, groaning, clicking, with great fusillades of thumps like cannon-fire as schools of big startled fish sped out of their way. The water grew warmer; jade-green, translucent. Glancing down, Will saw far below him the last signs of an old wreck. Only stumps remained of the masts and the raised decks, all eaten away by shipworms. From the mounded sand sifting over the hull an ancient cannon jutted, lumpy with coral, and two white skulls grinned up at Will. Killed by pirates, perhaps, he thought: destroyed, like too many men, neither by the Dark nor the Light but by their own kind. . . .

Porpoises played above their heads; great grey sharks cruised and turned, glancing curiously down as the two Old Ones flashed by. Down and down they went, to the twilight zone, that dim-lit layer of the ocean where only a little of the day can reach; where all the fish—long slender fish with great mouths, strange flattened fish with telescopic eyes—glowed with a cold light of their own. Then they were down in the deep sea, that covers more of the surface of the earth than any land or grass or tree, mountain or desert; in the cold dark where no normal man may see or survive. This was a region of fear and treachery, where every fish ate every other fish, where life was made only of fierce attack and the terror of desperate flight. Will saw huge toad-like fish with bright-tipped fishing-lines curving up from their backs, to hang cruelly alluring over wide mouths bristling with teeth. He saw a dreadful creature that seemed all mouth, a vast mouth like a funnel with a lid, and a puny body dwindling into a long whiplash tail. Beside it, the body of another began to swell horribly, as a big fish, struggling, disappeared inside the trap-like mouth. Will shuddered.

"No light," he said to Merriman, as they flashed onwards. "No joy in anything. Nothing but fear."

"This is not the world of men," Merriman said. "It is Tethys' world."

Even in the darkest sea they knew they were observed and escorted all the way, by subjects of Tethys invisible even to an Old One's eye. News came to the Lady of the Sea long, long before anyone might approach. She had her own ways. Older than the land, older than the Old Ones, older than all men, she ruled her kingdom of waves as she had since the world began: alone, absolute.

They came to a great crack in the bed of the sea, an abyss deeper than all the ocean deeps. A fine red mud covered the ocean floor. Though they had left all vestige of daylight long behind, miles above their heads, yet there was light of another kind in the black water, by which they could see as the creatures of the deep water saw. Eyes watched them from the darkness, from cracks and crevices. They were reaching the place for which they were bound.

As Will and Merriman slowed their rushing course, there in the lost places of the ocean, they could sense all these watchers around them, but slowly, vaguely, as if in a dream. And when at last the sea brought them to Tethys, they could not see her at all. She was a presence merely, she was the sea itself, and they spoke to her reverently, in the Old Speech.

"Welcome," said Tethys to them out of the darkness of the deeps of her sea. "Welcome to you, Old Ones of the earth. I have seen none of your kind for some little time now, for some fifteen centuries or so."

"And then it was I," Merriman said, smiling.

"And then indeed it was you, hawk," said she. "And one other, greater, with you, but this is not he, I think."

"I am new on the earth, madam, but I bring you my deep respect," said Will.

"Ah . . . ." Tethys said. "Aaaaah. . . ." And her sigh was the sighing of the sea.

"Hawk," she said then. "Why have you come again, this hard voyaging?"

"To beg a favour, lady," Merriman said.

"Of course," she said. "It is always so."

"And to bring a gift," he said.

"Ah?" There was a slight stirring in the shadows of the deep, like a gentle swell on the sea.

Will turned his head to Merriman in surprise; he had not known of any gift-bringing, though he realised now how proper it must be. Merriman drew from his sleeve a rolled piece of paper, a glimmering cylinder in the gloom; he unrolled it, and Will saw that it was Barney's drawing of Trewissick. He peered closer, curious, and saw a pen-and-ink sketch, rough but lively; the background of harbour and houses was no more than lightly outlined, and Barney had given all his attention to a detailed drawing in the foreground of a single fishing-boat and a patch of rippled sea. He had even drawn in the name on the boat's stern: she was called the *White Lady*.

Merriman held the drawing at arm's length, and released it into the sea; instantly it vanished into the shadow. There was a pause, then a soft laugh from Tethys. She sounded pleased.

"So the fishermen do not forget," she said. "Even after so long, some do not forget."

"The power of the sea will never change," Will said softly. "Even men recognise that. And these are islanders."

"And these are islanders." Tethys played with the words. "And they are my people, if any are."

"They do as they have always done," Merriman said. "They go out to the sea for fish at the going down of the sun, and with the dawn they return again. And once every year, when spring is full and summer lies ahead, they make for you, for the White Lady, a green figure of branches and leaves, and cast it down as a gift."

"The Greenwitch," Tethys said. "It has been born again already, this is the season. It will be here soon." A coldness came into the voice that filtered from the shadows. "What is this favour you ask, hawk? The Greenwitch is mine."

"The Greenwitch has always been yours, and always will. But because its understanding is not as great as your own, it has made the mistake of taking into its possession something that belongs to the Light."

"That has nothing to do with me," Tethys said.

A faint light seemed to glimmer from the blue-black shadow in which she was hidden, and all around them lights began to glow and flash from the fish and sea-creatures waiting there, watching. Will saw the dangling bait-stars over great gaping mouths; strings of round lights like port-holes running the length of strange slender fish. In the far distance he saw an odd cluster of lights of different colours, that seemed to belong to some bigger creature hidden in the shadow. He shivered, fearful of this alien element in which by enchantment they briefly breathed and swam.

"The Wild Magic has neither allies nor enemies," Merriman said coldly. "This you know. If you may not help us, yet it is not right for you to hinder us either, for in so doing you give aid to the Dark. And if the Greenwitch keeps that which it has found, the Dark will be very much strengthened."

"A poor argument," Tethys said. "You mean simply that the Light will then fail to gain an advantage. But I am not permitted to help either Light or Dark to gain any advantage. . . . You speak deviously, my friend."

"The White Lady sees everything," Merriman said, with a soft sad humility in his tone that startled Will, until he realised that it was no more than a delicate reminder of their gift.

"Ha." There was a flicker of amusement in the voice of the shadow. "We will have a bargain, Old Ones," Tethys said. "You may in my name try to persuade the Greenwitch to give up this . . . something . . . that is of such value to you. Before the creature comes to the depths, this is a matter between it and you. I shall not interfere, and the Dark may not interfere either, in my realm."

"Thank you, madam!" Will said, in quick delight.

But the voice went on, without pause, "This shall be only until the Greenwitch turns, to come to the deep sea. As it always comes, each year, to its proper home, to me . . . and after that time, Old Ones, anything that is in its possession is lost to you. You may not follow. None may follow. You may not return here, then, even by the spell which brings you here today. Should the Greenwitch choose to bring your secret down to the deeps, then in the deeps for ever it shall remain."

Merriman made as if to speak again, but the voice from the darkness was cold. "That is all. Go now."

"Madam—" Merriman said.

"Go!" Rage filled the voice of Tethys suddenly. There was a great flashing and roaring in the depths, all round them; strong currents rose, tugging at their limbs; fish and eels darted wildly round them in all directions, and out of the distant shadow a great shape came. It was the dark thing that carried within it the bright lights that Will had seen; nearer and nearer they came, looming larger and larger, white and purple and green, glaring out of a swelling black mass as high as a house. And Will saw with chill horror that the thing was a giant squid, one of the great monsters of the deep, huge and terrible. Each of its waving suckered tentacles was many times longer than his own height; he knew that it could move as fast as lightning, and that the tearing bite of its dreadful beak-like mouth could have annihilated either of them in a single instant. Fearful, he groped for a spell to destroy it.

"No!" said Merriman instantly into his mind. "Nothing will harm us here, whatever the danger may seem. The Lady of the Sea is, I think, merely . . . encouraging . . . us to leave." He swept a low, exaggerated bow to the shadows of the deep. "Our thanks, and our homage, lady," he called in a strong clear voice, and then with Will beside him he swept up and away, past the looming black shape of the huge squid, away to the great open green ocean, the way that they had come.

"We must go to the Greenwitch," he said to Will. "There is no time to lose."

"If there are the two of us," Will cried to him as they swept along, "and we work on the Greenwitch the spell of Mana and the spell of Reck and the spell of Lir, will it give up the manu-script to us?"

"That must come afterwards," called Merriman. "But those

spells will command it to listen, and hear, for only they harness the magic with which the Greenwitch was made."

They flashed through the sea like bars of light, out of the deep cold, up to the tropic warmth, back to the cold waters of Cornwall. But when they came to the place, beneath the waves beating their long swells against Kemare Head, the Greenwitch was not there. No sign remained. It had gone.

CHAPTER EIGHT

WHEN SIMON AND JANE ARRIVED BACK AT THE COTTAGE, THEY found Fran Stanton setting out plates on the dining-room table. "Hi," she said. "Want some lunch? Mrs Penhallow had to leave, but she made some great-looking Cornish pasties."

"I can smell them," Simon said hungrily.

"Lovely," said Jane. "Did you have a good time, where you went?"

"We didn't go far," Mrs Stanton said. "St Austell, round there. Clay-pits and factories and that sort of thing." She wrinkled her friendly face. "Still, after all that's what Bill came over for. And there's a real magic about those big white clay pyramids, and the pools so quiet at the bottom of them. Such green water.... Are you having fun? What's everyone doing?"

"Will and Great-Uncle Merry went for a walk. Barney's over at the Grey House with Captain Toms. We're supposed to go there too this afternoon, the captain wants us all to stay for supper," Jane said, boldly improvising. "That is if you don't mind."

"Perfect," Fran Stanton said. "Bill and I shan't be eating

here anyway—I left him seeing some guy near St Austell, and I have to go back tonight to pick him up. This afternoon I came back just to be lazy. Let's eat—and you can tell me all about that Greenwitch deal I wasn't allowed to watch, Jane."

So Jane, with some difficulty, gave a description of the making of the Greenwitch as of a gay all-night party, an outing for the local girls, while Simon wolfed down Cornish pasties and tried not to catch her eye. Mrs Stanton listened happily, shaking her blonde head in admiration.

"It's just wonderful the way these old customs are kept up," she said. "And I think it's great they wouldn't let a foreigner watch. So many of our Indians back home, they let the white man in to watch their native dances, and before you know it the whole thing's just a tourist trap."

"I'm glad you weren't offended," Jane said. "We were afraid—"

"Oh no no no," said Mrs Stanton. "Why, I've already got enough material to give a great paper on this trip to my travel group back home. We have this club, you see, it meets once a month and at each meeting someone gives a little talk, with slides, on somewhere she's been. This is the first time," she added a trifle wistfully, "I shall have had anywhere unusual to talk about—except Jamaica, and everyone else has been there too."

Afterwards Jane said to Simon, as they scrambled down towards the harbour, "She's rather sweet really. I'm glad she'll have us to talk about to her club."

"The natives and their quaint old customs," Simon said.

"Come on, you aren't even a native. You're one of they furriners from London."

"But I'm not so much *outside* it all as she is. Not her fault. She just comes from such a long way away, she isn't plugged in. Like all those people who go to the museum and look at the

86

grail and say, oh, how wonderful, without the least idea of what it really is."

"You mean people who used to look at it, when it was there."

"Oh lord. Yes."

"Well anyway," said Jane, "we'd be the same as Mrs Stanton if we were in her country."

"Of course we would, that's not the point. . . ."

They bickered amiably as they crossed the quay and started up the hill towards the Grey House. Pausing to get her breath, Jane looked back the way they had come. All at once she clutched the wall beside her, and stood there, staring.

"Simon!"

"What is it?"

"Look!"

Down in the harbour, in the very centre of the quay, was the painter, the man of the Dark. He sat on a folding stool before an easel, with a knapsack open on the ground beside him, and he was painting. There was no urgency in his movements; he sat there tranquil and unhurried, dabbing at the canvas. Two visitors paused behind him to watch; he paid them no attention, but went serenely on with his work.

"Just *sitting* there!" Simon said, astounded.

"It's a trick. It must be. Perhaps he has an accomplice, someone off doing things for him while he attracts our attention."

Simon said slowly, "There was no sign of anyone else having been in the caravan. And the farm looked as if it had been empty for years."

"Let's go and tell the captain."

But there was no need to tell him. At the Grey House, they found Barney perched in a small high room overlooking the harbour, studying the painter through Captain Toms' largest telescope. The old man himself, having let them in, remained below. "This foot of mine," he said ruefully, "isn't too grand at climbing up and down stairs."

"But I bet you he could see as much with his eyes shut, if he wanted to, as I can through this thing," Barney said, squinting down the telescope with one eye closed and his face screwed up. "He's special. You know? Just like Gumerry. They're the same kind."

"But what kind is that, I wonder?" Jane said thoughtfully.

"Who knows?" Barney stood up, stretching. "A weird kind. A super kind. The kind that belongs to the Light."

"Whatever that is."

"Yes. Whatever that is."

"Hey Jane, look at this!" Simon was bending to the eyepiece of the telescope. "It's fantastic, like being right on top of him. You can practically count his eyelashes."

"I've been staring at that face so long I could draw it from memory," Barney said.

Simon was glued to the lens, entranced. "It's as good as being able to hear anything he says. You might even be able to lip-read. You can see every single little change of expression."

"That's right," Barney said. He looked casually out of the window; breathed on the pane; drew a little face in the misted patch of glass, and then rubbed it out again. "The view of his face is terrific. The only trouble is, there's no view of his painting at all."

Jane had taken her turn at the telescope now. She gazed nervously at the face caught out of the distance by the powerful lens: a dark-browed face, grim with concentration, framed by the long unruly hair. "Well yes, from this angle of course you're just looking at the back of the easel, looking down at his face over the top of the canvas. But that's not important, is it?"

"It is if you're an artist, like Barney," Simon said. He clasped his head, striking an extravagant artistic pose.

"Ha ha," said Barney, with heavy patience. "It's not just that. I thought the picture might be important."

"Why?"

"I don't know. Captain Toms did ask me what he was painting."

"What did he say when you said you couldn't see?"

"He didn't say anything."

"Well then."

"Your painter doesn't change his expression one bit, does he?" Jane was still peering. "Just sits there glaring at the canvas. Funny."

"Not very funny," Simon said. "He's a glaring sort of man."

"No, I mean it's funny he doesn't look anywhere else. If you watch Mother when she's painting a landscape, you can see her eyes going up and down all the time. Flickering. From whatever it is she's painting, down to the picture and then back again. But he's not doing that at all."

"Let me have another look." Barney edged her aside and stared eagerly into the lens, grabbing his blonde forelock out of the way. "You know, you're right. Why didn't I notice that?" He thumped his knee with his fist.

"I still don't see what there is to get excited about," Simon said mildly.

"Well, perhaps it's nothing. But let's go and tell Captain Toms anyway."

They clattered down three flights of stairs, and into the book-lined living-room at the front of the house. Rufus stood up and waved his tail at them. Captain Toms was standing beside one of the bookcases, gazing at a small book open in his hands. He looked up as they rushed to him, and closed the book.

"What news, citizens?" he said.

Barney said, "He's still sitting there painting. But Jane just noticed something, he's not painting from life. I mean he just looks at the canvas, without even glancing at anything else at all."

"So he might just as well be painting in his caravan as painting here," said Simon, his mind now in gear. "So, he can't really be here to paint, he must be here for some other reason."

"That may be quite right," Captain Toms said. He parted the books on the nearest shelf, carefully, and slipped his volume back. "And then again it may not be quite right."

"What do you mean?" Jane said.

"The painting and the other reason may be one and the same thing. The only trouble is," Captain Toms stared up at his books as if willing them to speak, "I can't for the life of me work out what that thing is all about."

* * *

Hour after hour they watched, in turn. At length, after an early supper that might equally have been called a late tea, Jane and Simon sat again in the book-clothed living-room with Captain Toms. He puffed contentedly at a friendly-smelling pipe, grey hair wisping out round his bald head like the tonsure of some genial old monk.

"It'll be dark soon," Jane said, looking out at the orange-red sunset sky. "He'll have to stop painting then."

"Yes, but he's still at it," Simon said, "or Barney would have come down from the eyrie." He prowled round the room, peering at the pictures that hung between bookcases. "I remember these ships from last year. The *Golden Hind* . . . the *Mary and Ellen* . . . the *Lottery*—that's a funny name for a ship."

"So it is," said Captain Toms. "But suitable. A lottery is a gamble, of sorts—and she was owned by gamblers, of sorts. She was a famous smugglers' ship."

"Smugglers!" Simon's eyes gleamed.

"A regular trade it was in Cornwall, two hundred years ago. Smuggling . . . they didn't even call it that, they called it fair-trading. Fast little boats they had, beautiful sailors. Many a fair-trader's boat was built right here in Trewissick." The old man gazed absently down at his pipe, turning it in his fingers, his eyes distant. "But the tale of the *Lottery* is a black tale, about an ancestor of mine I sometimes wish I could forget. Though it's better to remember. . . . Out of Polperro, the *Lottery* was, a beauty before the wind. Her crew had years of fair-trading, never caught, until one day east of here a Revenue cutter came up with her, both ships fired on one another, and a Revenue man was killed. Well now, killing was a different thing from smuggling. So all the crew of the *Lottery* became hunted men. Tisn't hard to escape capture in Cornwall, and for a while they were all safe. And they might have been for longer, but one of the crew, Roger Toms, gave himself up to the Revenue and turned King's Evidence, telling them it was a shipmate of his called Tom Potter that fired the dire shot."

"And Roger Toms was your ancestor," Jane said.

"He was, poor misguided fellow. The folk of Polperro took him and set him on a boat bound for the Channel Isles, so he shouldn't be able to give evidence against Tom Potter in court. But the Revenue brought him back again, and Tom Potter was arrested, and tried at the Old Bailey in London, and hanged."

"And wasn't Potter guilty?" Simon said.

"No-one knows, to this day. Polperro folk claimed he was innocent—some even said Roger Toms fired the shot himself. But they may just have been protecting one of their own, for Tom Potter was born in Polperro, but Roger Toms was a Trewissick man."

Simon said severely, "He shouldn't have sneaked on his shipmate, even if Potter did do it. That's like murder."

"So it was," Captain Toms said gently. "So it was. And

Roger Toms never dared set foot in Cornwall again, from that day until the day he died. But no-one ever knew his real motives. Some Trewissick folk say that Potter was guilty, and that Toms gave him up for the sake of all the wives and children, thinking it sure that unless the one guilty man were accused, sooner or later all the crew of the *Lottery* would be taken and hanged. But most think black thoughts of him. He is the town's shame, not forgotten even yet." He looked out of the window at the darkening sky, and the blue eyes in the round cherubic face were suddenly hard. "The very best and the very worst have come out of Cornwall. And come into her, too."

Jane and Simon stared at him, puzzled. Before they could say anything, Barney came into the room.

"Your turn, Simon. Captain, d'you think I could go and get some more of that super cake?"

"Hungry work, watching," said Captain Toms solemnly. "Of course you may."

"Thank you." Barney paused for a moment at the door, glancing round the room. "Watch this," he said, and he reached for a switch and turned on the lights.

"Goodness!" said Jane, blinking in the sudden brightness. "It's got really dark. We hadn't noticed, we were talking."

"And he's still sitting out there," Barney said.

"Still? In the dark? How can he paint in the dark?"

"Well, he is. He may not be painting what's in front of him, but he's still putting paint on that canvas, cool as a cucumber. The moon's up, it's only a half-moon but it gives enough of a glimmer that you can still see him through the glass. I tell you, he must be stark raving nuts."

Simon said, "You don't remember the caravan. He's not nuts. He's from the Dark."

He went out of the room and up the stairs. Shrugging, Barney headed for the kitchen to fetch his cake.

Jane said, "Captain Toms, when will Gumerry be back?"

"When he has found out what he went to find out. Don't worry. They will come straight to us." Captain Toms heaved himself to his feet, reaching for his stick. "I think I might perhaps take a look through that telescope too, now, if you'll excuse me for a moment, Jane."

"Can you manage?"

"Oh yes, thank you. I just take my time." He hobbled out, and Jane went to kneel on the window-seat, staring out at the harbour. A wind was rising, out there; she could hear it beginning to whine softly in the window-frames. She thought: he'll get cold out there soon, the painter from the Dark. Why does he stay there? *What's he doing?*

The wind grew. The moon went out. The sky was dark, and Jane could no longer see the pattern of clouds that had been dimly visible before. All at once she realised that she could hear the sea. Normally the soft swish of the waves against the harbour wall made a constant low music that was part of life; being always there, it was scarcely heard. But now the sound of each wave was distinct; she could hear each smack and splash. The sea, like the wind, was rising.

Simon and Captain Toms came back into the room. Jane saw their reflections ghostly in the window, and turned.

"Can't see him any more," Simon said. "There's no light. But I don't think he's gone."

Jane looked at Captain Toms. "What should we do?"

The old sailor's face was troubled, creased with thinking; he tilted his head, listening to the wind. "I shall wait a little to see what the weather does, for more reasons than you might think. After that—after that, we shall see."

Barney appeared in the doorway, munching a large piece of bright yellow cake.

"Good gracious," said Jane brightly, to stop herself listening to the sea, "you must have eaten the whole plateful by now."

"Mmmmf," Barney said. He swallowed. "Do you know, he's still there?"

"What?" They stared at him.

"I haven't just been stuffing myself in the kitchen. I popped out round the back and crossed the road in front here, to look down from the harbour wall—thought he might see the light if I opened the front door. And he's still there! Right where he was. He really must be cracked, you know, Simon. Dark or not. I mean he's sitting there in the darkness at his easel, still painting. Still painting, in the pitch dark! He's got some sort of light, it's only by the glow that you can see he's there. But all the same, really—"

Captain Toms sat down abruptly in an armchair. He said, half to himself, "I don't like it. It makes no sense. I try to see, and there is only shadow. . . ."

"The wind's making a lot more noise now," Jane said. She shivered.

"Out there, you can hear the waves really crashing against the headland," Barney said cheerfully. He crammed the last of his cake into his mouth.

Simon said, "Is there going to be a storm, captain?"

The old man gave no answer. He sat hunched in his chair, staring into the empty fireplace. Rufus, who had been lying peaceably on the hearth rug, got up and licked his hand, whining. A sudden gust of wind whistled in the chimney, and rattled the front door. Jane jumped.

"Oh dear," she said. "I hope Gumerry's all right. I wish we'd arranged for some great big signal to bring him back if we wanted him. Like Indians and smoke signals."

"Just a fire, you'd need, now it's dark," Barney said. "A beacon fire."

"In these parts," Captain Toms said abstractedly, "beacon fires date back as far as the men who have always lighted them. A warning, from the beginning of time. . . ." He leaned forwards, his hands clasped together over the top of his carved walking-stick, and he gazed unseeingly in front of him as if he were looking back into endless centuries, oblivious of the room and the children in it. When he spoke again, the voice seemed younger, clearer, stronger, so that they paused in astonishment where they stood.

"And when last the Dark came rising in this land," Captain Toms said, "it came from the sea, and the men of Cornwall lit beacon fires everywhere to warn of its coming. From Estols to Trecobben to Carn Brea the warning fires sprang, from St Agnes to Belovely and St Bellarmine's Tor, and on out to Cadbarrow and Rough Tor and Brown Willy. And the last was at Vellan Druchar, and there the Light gave battle to the Dark. The forces of the Dark were driven back to the sea, and might have escaped that way, to attack again. But the Lady brought home a west wind, that threw all their hope of escape dry upon the shore, and so the forces of the Dark were vanquished, for that time. Yet the first of the Old Ones gave prophecy, that once more from that same sea and shore the Dark should one day come rising."

He stopped abruptly, and they were left staring at him.

Simon said huskily, at last, "Is . . . is the Dark rising now?"

"I don't know," Captain Toms said simply, in his normal voice. "I think not, Simon. It is all but impossible for them to rise yet. But in that case, something else is happening that I do not understand at all." He stood up, leaning on the arm of the chair. "I think perhaps it is time that I went out there, to see what I can see."

"We'll come with you," said Simon at once.

"Are you sure?"

"To tell the truth," Jane said, "whatever happens out there, I think we'd rather come with you than stay on our own."

"Too true," Barney said.

Captain Toms smiled. "Get your jackets, then. Rufus, you stay here. Stay."

Leaving the red dog resentful on the hearth rug, they went out of the Grey House and crept down the hill, slowly, at the captain's painful pace. At the bottom, where the downhill road joined the quay, the old man drew them gently into the shadow of a warehouse at the back of the harbour. Standing huddled there, whipped by the wind blowing in from the sea, they could see the painter from the Dark not twenty yards from them, at the edge of the sea; the light around him made him clear.

As Jane looked at him for the first time, she gasped, and heard the same instinctive strangled sound from the others. For the painter had no flashlight to make the pool of brightness that surrounded him. The light came from his painting.

Green and blue and yellow it glowed there in the darkness, in great writhing seething patterns like a nest of snakes. Seeing it now for the first time Jane felt an instant dreadful revulsion from the picture, its shape and colour and mood, yet she could not take her eyes from it. The man was still painting, even now. With the wind grabbing at his clothes, and tilting his easel towards him so that he had to hold it still with one hand, he was yet daubing away frenziedly with a brush full of these strange horrible colours, and to Jane's bemused eye it seemed that all the colours came from the brush itself without the least pause for taking up new paint.

"It's horrible!" Barney said violently. He spoke with great force, unthinking, but the wind whipped the words out of his mouth as soon as they were uttered. The painter, standing to windward, would not have heard him even if he had yelled at the top of his lungs.

"Now I see!" Captain Toms suddenly thumped his stick on the ground, staring at the picture. "That's it! Now I understand! He has painted his spells! Mana and Reck and Lir . . . the power is all in the picture! I had forgotten it could be done. Now I see, now I see . . . but too late. Too late. . . ."

Jane said fearfully into the wind, "Too late?"

And the wind rose howling in their ears, lashing at their faces, flinging salt spray into their eyes. There was no rain, nor any lightning or thunder; they heard only the wind and the crashing of the sea. They staggered backwards against the wall, pinned to it by the gale; out on the quay the painter hunched his broad shoulders forwards, leaning into the wind to hold himself upright. He flung away his brush; paints and papers rushed away from him and were gone on the wind; all that he held was the strange glimmering canvas. He raised it above his head, and shouted some words in a tongue the children did not understand.

And suddenly they heard a sound like nothing they had ever heard from the sea before: a great sucking, hissing noise, echoing from side to side of the little harbour. The wind died away. There was all at once a strong, very strong smell of the sea: a smell not of decay but of foam, and waves, and fish and seaweed and tar and wet sand and shells.

For a second the moon sailed out from behind a broken cloud, and they saw a great sideways impossible wave roll back to each side of the harbour. And up out of the water came a towering dark shape, twice as high as a man, looming over the painter, bringing with it even more overpoweringly the tremendous smell of the sea.

The painter flung up his arms holding the canvas, thrusting it at the great black shape, and cried out in a voice that cracked with strain, "Stay! Stay, I charge you!"

Captain Toms spoke softly, wonderingly, half to himself. "Watch for the Greenwitch," he said.

CHAPTER NINE

THEY HUDDLED IN THE DARK WAREHOUSE DOORWAY, WATCHING. No wind blew now, and the sudden stillness was unnerving, broken only by the rumbling waves. The murmur of passing motor-cars came now and then from the main road higher in the village, but the children did not heed them. Nothing in the world seemed to exist but this thing that loomed before them, rising higher each moment out of the swaying sea.

The thing could not be clearly seen. It had no features, no outline, no recognisable shape. They perceived it only as a great mass of black absolute darkness, blotting out all light or starglimmer, rearing up over the weird glowing patch that marked the man of the Dark. It was, Jane thought suddenly, far larger than the image of leaves and branches that she had seen cast down into the sea from the point of Kemare Head. And yet, she thought again, the Greenwitch had seemed huge in the dark of that night, rearing up, waiting, shadowed by the flickering beacon fire. . . .

The painter said in a loud clear voice, "Greenwitch!"

Simon felt Barney shiver convulsively, and he moved closer to him. A hand briefly, gratefully, clutched his arm.

"Greenwitch! Greenwitch!"

A great voice came out of the towering massive darkness. It seemed to fill all the night; a voice like the sea, full of shifting music. It said, "Why do you call me out?"

The painter lowered his dreadful canvas. The light in it was beginning gradually to fade. "I have need of you."

"I am the Greenwitch," the voice said wearily. "I am made for the sea, I am of the sea. I can do nothing for you."

"I have a small favour to ask," the painter said: sweetly, ingratiatingly, but with a strain in his voice as if it would crack into a thousand glittering fragments.

The voice said, "You are of the Dark. I feel it. I am not permitted to have any dealings with either the Dark or the Light. It is the Law."

The painter said quickly, "But you have taken something that the Law does not permit you to take. You know it. You have a part of one of the ancient Things of Power, that you should not have, that no creature of the Wild Magic should have. Greenwitch, you must give it to me."

The sea-voice of the blackness cried out as if in pain, "No! It is mine! It is my secret! My secret!" And Jane flinched, for suddenly it was the voice of her dream: plaintive, crying, a child's complaint.

The painter said fiercely, "It is not yours."

"It is my secret!" cried the Greenwitch, and the mass of black darkness seemed to rise and swell. "I guard it, none shall touch it. It is mine, for always!"

At once the painter dropped his tone into gentleness, a soft wheedling. "Greenwitch, Greenwitch, child of Tethys, child of Poseidon, child of Neptune—what need have you of a secret, in the deeps?"

"As much need as you," the Greenwitch said.

"Your home is in the deeps." The painter was still gentle,

persuasive. "There is no need for such secrets there. That is no place for such a thing, woven of different spells that you know nothing of."

The huge voice of the darkness said obstinately, almost pettishly, "It is mine. I found it."

The painter's voice, shaking, began to rise. "Fool! Wild fool! How dare you play with things of the High Magic!"

The light was fading faster out of his painting now; the children could see nothing around it but the blackness of the Greenwitch against the faint grey glimmer of sky and sea. There were only these two voices, ringing through the empty harbour.

"You are a made creature only, you will do as I say!" Arrogance sharpened the man's tone, gave it an edge of command. "Give the thing to me, at once, before the Dark shall blast you out of this world!"

The children felt Captain Toms gently but urgently drawing them all back against the wall, into a corner almost cut off from the spot where the two figures confronted one another on the quay. Nervously they moved as they were told.

From the blackness that was the Greenwitch came a hair-raising sound: a long low lamenting, like a moan, rising and falling in a mumbling whine. Then it stopped, and the creature began muttering to itself, broken words that they could not make out. Then there was silence for a moment and all at once it said very clearly, "You have not the full power of the Dark."

"Now! I command you!" The painter's voice was shrill.

"You have not the full power of the Dark," the Greenwitch said again, with a growing, wondering confidence. "When the Dark comes rising, it is not as one man, but as a terrible great blackness filling the sky and the earth. I see it, my mother shows me. But you are alone. You were sent by the Dark with one small mission only, and you gamble now to make yourself a great Lord, one of the masters. By completing one of the

Things of Power for yourself, you think to become great. But you are not great yet, *and you may not command me!*"

Softly, Captain Toms said, "Tethys has seen what we could not see."

"I have all the power required!" said the painter loudly. "Now, Greenwitch, now! Do as the Dark demands!"

The Greenwitch began to make a new sound, a low rumbling so ominous that the children shrank back against the wall. It was somewhere between the growl of a dog and the purring of a cat, and it said, *Beware, beware. . . .*

The painter cried out furiously, "By the spell of Mana and the spell of Reck and the spell of Lir!" and they saw by the last faint glow that he swung up his canvas and its luminous painted magic over his head again, facing the blackness of the Greenwitch. But he could do nothing. The rumbling from the Greenwitch rose into a roar, the air was tight with rebellion and fear, and Jane heard in her mind over and over again the cry *Leave me alone! Leave me alone! Leave me alone!* and never knew whether it had been cried aloud or not.

They were conscious of nothing but a great seething. Resentful fury roared in their ears, throbbing with the slow thunder of waves against rock. And suddenly the whole world was luminous with green light, as for one terrible moment the Greenwitch in all its wild power loomed out of the sky, every live detail clear with a brilliance they never afterwards mentioned even to one another. With a shriek the painter flung himself backwards, and fell to the ground. And the Greenwitch, crying rage from a great mouth, spread terrible arms wide as if to engulf the whole village—and disappeared. It did not go down into the sea. It did not vanish like a burst balloon. It faded, like smoke, dissipating into nothing. And they felt no sense of release from fear, but a greater tension as if there were a storm in the air.

Barney whispered, "Has it gone?"

"No," Captain Toms said gravely. "It is all through the village. It is with us and around us. It is angry and it is everywhere, and there is great danger. I must take you home at once. Merry had good reasons for choosing those cottages—they are as safe as the Grey House, in the protection of the Light."

Barney was looking at the still figure on the quay. He said fearfully, "Is he dead?"

"That is not possible," Captain Toms said quietly. He looked down at the painter. The man lay on his back, breathing evenly, his long hair spread like a black pool around his head. His eyes were closed, but there was no sign of injury. He looked as though he were asleep.

From the road leading into the harbour they heard the engine of a car, growing closer, rounding the corner. Simon stepped out to wave it down, but there was no need. As the car's lights swung on to the group on the quay it slowed abruptly, brakes screaming, and pulled to a halt. From behind the blazing head lamps an American voice called, "Hey! What goes on?"

"It's the Stantons!" The children rushed to the car doors, and two puzzled figures climbed out. Captain Toms turned quickly; his voice was clear and commanding.

"Evening—you've picked a good time to appear. We've just found this fellow lying here, on our way to the cottage—looks as if a car's knocked him down. Hit and run, I reckon."

Bill Stanton knelt beside the prostrate painter and felt for his heart; raised one eyelid; gently felt along his arms and legs. "He's alive . . . no blood anywhere . . . no obvious breaks . . . maybe it's a heart attack, not a car. What should we do? Is there an ambulance here?"

Captain Toms shook his head. "No ambulance in Trewissick,

we're not too good for emergencies. And only one policeman, with a motor-bike. . . . You know, Mr Stanton, the best thing we could do is get him in your car, and you drive him to the hospital in St Austell. Poor fellow might be dead by the time we get P.C. Tregear out."

"He's right," said Fran Stanton, her soft voice concerned. "Let's do that, Bill."

"Fine by me." Mr Stanton looked round the quayside, his eyes searching, quickly efficient. "We'll have to be very careful lifting him. . . . I wonder . . . ah!" He prodded Simon, nearest him. "See that pile of planks over there? Two of you kids bring one, quick."

In a struggling group they slid the painter on to the narrow plank; then, with slow lifting and tilting, manoeuvred it to leave him lying on the back seat of the car.

"Do up the seat belts round him, Frannie," said Mr Stanton, climbing back into the driver's seat. "He should be okay. . . . Will you call the policeman, captain, and have him follow us? Shouldn't like anyone to think it was us knocked the guy down."

"Yes, of course."

Fran Stanton paused with the car door open. "Where's Will?"

Her husband took his hand off the ignition key. "That's right, it's late. He and Merry can't still be out walking. Where is he, kids?"

They stared at him, speechless.

The brightness died out of Bill Stanton's amiable round face; in its place came suspicion and concern. "Hey now, what is all this? What's going on here? Where's Will?"

Captain Toms cleared his throat. "He—" he began.

"Nothing to worry about, Uncle Bill," said Will, behind them. "Here I am."

CHAPTER TEN

"VERY GOOD," SAID MERRIMAN, WATCHING, AS THE STANTONS' car hummed round the corner from the harbour and away into the main village street. "They should just have time to get clear."

"You make it sound as though somebody was going to drop a bomb," Simon said.

Jane said nervously, "Gumerry? What's going to happen?"

"Nothing, to you. Come along." Merriman swung round and began striding fast and long-legged across the quay towards the cottages; the children scurried after.

"See you later, Merry!" Captain Toms called.

They stopped, turning in consternation; he was beginning to limp back to the Grey House. "Captain? Aren't you coming with us?"

"Captain Toms!"

"Come along," Merriman said without feeling, and pushed them before him. They shot him quick glances of irritation and reproach. Only Will marched along without sign of emotion.

"I'm so glad you're back." Jane slipped round to her great-uncle's side. "Please, what's going to happen? Really?"

Merriman glanced down at her from his deep-shadowed eyes, without slackening his pace. "The Greenwitch is abroad. All the power of the Wild Magic, which is without discipline or pattern, is let loose tonight in this place. The power of the Light, since we have so arranged it, will give protection to the cottages and to the Grey House. But elsewhere . . . Trewissick is under possession, this night. It will not be an easy place." His deep voice was tense and grave, filling them with alarm; they trotted nervously at his side and up the winding zig-zag alleys and stairs to the cottage door. Then they fell into the lighted room like mice diving below-ground from a hunting owl.

Simon swallowed, regaining his breath, feeling slightly ashamed of his haste. He said belligerently to Will, "Where were you?"

"Talking to people," Will said.

"Well, what did you find out? You were gone long enough."

"Nothing much," Will said mildly. "Nothing but what hasn't already happened."

"Wasn't much point in your going then, was there?"

Will laughed. "Not really."

Simon stared at him for a moment and then turned irritably away. Will glanced at Jane, and winked. She gave him a quick rueful grin, but studied him afterwards, behind his back. *Simon wanted to quarrel, and you wouldn't,* she thought. *You're like a grown-up, sometimes. Who are you, Will Stanton?*

She said, "Gumerry, what should we do? Would you like Simon and me to keep watch, upstairs?"

"I should like you all to go to bed," Merriman said. "It's late."

"Bed!" The outrage in Barney's voice was louder even than the others'. "But everything's just getting really exciting!"

"Exciting is one word for it." Merriman's bony face was grim. "Later you might have another. Do as you are told, please." There was a flicking edge to the words that did not inspire argument.

"Goodnight," Jane said meekly. "Goodnight, Will."

"See you in the morning, everyone," Will said casually, and he disappeared into the Stanton half of the house.

Jane shivered.

"What's the matter?" Simon said.

"Someone walked over my grave. . . . I don't know, perhaps I've caught a chill."

"I'll make you all a hot drink and bring it up," Merriman said.

Upstairs, Simon paused in the little corridor linking the bedrooms, clutching his head in a kind of despairing fierceness. "This is ludicrous! Crazy! One minute we're in the middle of some awful great . . . watching that, that *thing* . . . and then Gumerry turns up, and before you know it he's tucking us up with cups of cocoa."

Barney gave a huge yawn. "Well yes . . . but I'm . . . tired. . . ."

Jane shivered again. "I am too, I think. I don't know. I feel funny. As if—Can you hear a sort of buzzing noise, very faint, a long way off?"

"No," Simon said.

"I'm sleepy," Barney said. "G'night."

"I'm coming too," said Simon. He looked at Jane. "Are you going to be all right, on your own?"

"Well, if anything happens," Jane said, "I'm going to come running in to hide under your bed so fast you won't even see me."

Simon managed a small grin. "You do that. There's one thing certain, absolutely no-one is going to get any sleep tonight."

But when Merriman came tapping gently at Jane's bedroom door in a little while, there were three steaming mugs still on his tray. "I might have saved myself the effort," he said. "Simon and Barney are fast asleep already."

107

Jane was sitting in pyjamas and dressing-gown beside the window, looking out. She said, without turning round, "Have you magicked them?"

Merriman said softly, "No." Something in his voice made her turn, then. He was standing in the doorway, his eyes glittering out of black pools of shadow beneath the jutting white-wire eyebrows. He stood so tall in the low little room that his bushy white hair touched the ceiling. "Jane," he said. "Nothing has been done to any of you, or will be. I promised you that in the beginning. And no harm can come to you here. Remember that. You know me well enough, I do not put you into mortal danger, now or ever."

"I know. Of course I do," she said.

"Then sleep sound," Merriman said. He stretched out a long arm, and she reached out and touched his fingertips; it was like a bargain. "Here, have some cocoa. No potions in it, I promise. Just sugar."

Jane said automatically, "I've cleaned my teeth."

Merriman chuckled. "Then clean them again." He put down the mug and went out, closing the door.

Jane took her cocoa and sat beside the window again, warming her fingers on the hot smooth sides of the mug; the room was cold. She looked out of the window, but the reflection of the bedside lamp was in her way. Impulsively she reached out and switched it off, then sat waiting until her eyes grew accustomed to the dim-lit dark.

When at last she could see again, she did not believe what she saw.

From the cottage, high up there on the hillside above the sea, she had a clear view of all the harbour and much of the village. Here and there were pools of yellow light from the lamp-posts: two on the quayside, three across the harbour, up on the road past the Grey House; others, more distant, at points within the village. But the pools of light were small. All else was darkness. And in the darkness, wherever she looked, Jane could see things moving. At first she could tell herself that she was imagining it, for whenever she saw movement from the corner of an eye and shifted her gaze to stare, it was gone. She could never see it clearly, in direct view. But this did not last for long.

It was changed by a single figure of a man. He came up out of the water at the edge of the harbour, climbing a flight of stairs with a strange gliding motion.

He was dripping wet; his clothes clung to him, his long hair was plastered flat and dark round his face, and as he walked a trail of water dripped all round him and was left like a path. He walked slowly up towards the main street of Trewissick, looking neither to left nor right. When he came to the corner of the little canning factory, whose new extension jutted from the old brick buildings set higgledy-piggledy along the quay, the man in the wet clothes did not slow his pace, nor turn aside. He simply walked through the wall as if it had not been there, emerging in a second or two on the other side. Then he disappeared into the darkness of the main street.

Jane stared into the blackness. She said softly, desperately, "It's not true. It's not true."

The night was very still. Jane clutched her mug like a talisman of reality; then suddenly jumped so hard that she spilt half the cocoa on the window-sill. She had caught a movement right below her, at the cottage door. Hardly daring to look, she willed her eyes to move downwards, and saw two figures leaving the door. Merriman was unmistakable; though he was hooded and muffled in a long cloak, light from a street-lamp showed Jane the high brow and fierce beak-like nose. But it was a moment before she realised that the second figure, cloaked and hooded in the same way, was Will Stanton. She knew him only by a trick of his walk, which until then she would not have thought she could recognise.

They walked out unhurried into the middle of the quay. Jane felt a frenzied urge to throw open the window and shriek a warning, to bring them back from unknown perils, but she had known her strange great-uncle too long for that. He had never been like other men; he had always had unpredictable powers, seemed somehow larger than anyone they had ever known. He might even be causing these things.

"He is of the Light," said Jane aloud to herself, gravely, hearing the true impossible seriousness of the words for the first time.

Then she said thoughtfully, amending it a little, "They are of the Light." She looked at the smaller hooded figure, discovering in her mind a curious reluctance to believe that there was anything supernatural about Will. His cheerful round face, with the blue-grey eyes and straight mouse-brown hair, had seemed a subtly comforting image from the beginning of this adventure. There would be nothing very comforting about Will if he were like Merriman Lyon.

And then she forgot Merriman, Will and everything around her, for she caught sight of the lights.

They were the lights of a ship, out at sea: bright lights like stars, moving a little as with the waves. They swayed and bobbed out there in the darkness, but they were far too close in. Though they were clearly the lights of a ship of some size, they were close to the rocks of Kemare Head; dreadfully, dangerously close. She heard voices, crying faintly; one of them seemed to call: "Jack Harry's lights!" And forcing her gaze away from the sea she saw that the harbour was suddenly filled with people: fishermen, women, boys, running and waving and pointing out at the sea. They crowded past and around the still figures of Merriman and Will as if neither of them was there.

Then there seemed to Jane to be a strange blurring of the scene, a moment's vagueness; when her eyes cleared, everything was as it had been the moment before, and though she thought that the crowd of villagers seemed somehow different, in clothes and appearance, she could not be certain. Before she could think further, horror seemed to take hold of the crowd. An eerie flickering light grew over the harbour. And suddenly boats set about with great flaming torches were pouring in past the harbour wall, strange broad boats full of oarsmen, some bare-headed with flowing red hair, some wearing stubby helmets crested with a golden boar and jutting down into a fierce iron nose-guard over the face. The boats reached shallow water; the oarsmen leapt from their oars, seized swords and blazing torches and tumbled out, crowding, splashing, rushing ashore with blood-curdling yells that Jane could hear with dreadful clarity even through the closed window. The villagers scattered, screaming, fleeing in all directions; some few fought the invaders off with sticks and knives. But the red-headed men were intent on one thing only; they hewed and hacked with their swords, slicing at any they could catch with more fearsome brutality than Jane had ever believed possible in human beings. Blood ran bright over the quayside, and streamed down into the sea, clouding out dark and murky in the waves.

Jane stumbled to her feet, feeling sick, and turned away.

When she forced herself back to the window, shivering, the screams and yells had died almost to nothing. The last fugitives and howling invaders were racing out along the furthest roads, and an ominous red glow was rising all over the village, all over the sky. Trewissick was burning. Flames licked round the houses on the hill across the harbour, and glared bright red in the windows; in a great whoosh of fire the warehouse at the far side of the harbour burst into flames. Brick and stone seemed incomprehensibly to burn as fiercely as if they were wood.

Fumbling desperately with the catch, Jane flung open the window, and met a great crackling and roaring from the fire and the great billowing clouds of bright-lit smoke. The reflection of the flames danced on the water of the harbour. In her agitation it did not occur to Jane to notice that she did not smell burning, and felt no heat.

Down on the quayside, as if they saw nothing that had happened from the beginning, Will and Merriman stood cloaked and still.

"Gumerry!" Jane shrieked. She could think of nothing but that the fire might reach the cottages. "Gumerry!"

Then the noise outside in the sky was suddenly gone, altogether gone, and she heard her own voice, and found that what she had felt as a high tremendous scream was no more than a whisper. And as she sat watching, disbelieving, the flames died and disappeared, and the red glow in the sky faded away. There was no more blood, nor any trace of it, and everything in the harbour of Trewissick was as if the red-headed, ravening men from the sea had never come.

Somewhere, a dog howled into the night.

Cold, frightened, Jane clutched her dressing-gown tighter around her. She longed to fetch Simon, yet she could not take her eyes from the window. Still unmoving, the dark cloaked figures of Will and Merriman stood over the edge of the sea. They made no sign of having noticed anything that had happened.

There was a glimmering, glittering sheen on the water of the harbour, and Jane saw that over her head the moon had floated free of clouds. A different light brightened the world, cold but gentler: all was black and white and grey. And into it, out of the air, came a voice. It was not a man's voice, but thin and unearthly, chanting one sentence three times on one high heart-catching note.

The hour is come, but not the man.
The hour is come, but not the man.
The hour is come, but not the man.

Jane peered all round the harbour, but could see no-one: only the two unmoving figures below.

Again the dog howled somewhere unseen. Again she felt a strange buzzing, humming sound in the air, and then she began to hear other voices crying far off in the village.

"The *Lottery!* The *Lottery!*" she thought they cried. Then a man's voice, clearer, "The *Lottery* is taken!"

"Roger Toms! Roger Toms!"

"Hide them!"

"Bring them to the caves!"

"The Revenuers are coming!"

A woman sobbed: "Roger Toms, Roger Toms. . . ."

The harbour filled with people, milling about, anxiously staring out to sea, scurrying to and fro. This time Jane thought she could see faces in the crowd that were like the faces of Trewissick that she knew: Penhallows, Palks, Hoovers, Tregarrens, Thomases, all anxious, all perplexed, casting fearful glances both to land and sea. They seemed to have no real contact with one another; they were like sleep-walkers, sleep-runners, folk desperately turning about in a bad dream. And a great shriek went up from the whole crowd as the last spectre came rushing at them from the sea.

It was not horrible, yet it was more heart-stopping than any. It was a ship: a black ship, single-masted, square-rigged, with a dinghy behind. Silent and unnerving it came gliding into the harbour from the sea, scarcely touching the water, skimming the surface of the waves. It carried no crew. Not a single form moved anywhere on its black decks. And when it reached the land, it did not stop, but went on, sailing silently over harbour and rooftops and hill, away out of Trewissick, to the moors.

And as if the phantom ship had swept away with it all sign of life, the crowd vanished too.

Jane found she was clutching the edge of the window-sill so hard that her fingers hurt. She thought miserably: *this is why he wanted us to sleep. Safe and empty with a blanket over our minds, that's where he wanted us. And instead I am in the middle of more nightmares than I ever imagined could come in one night, and the worst nightmare of all is that I am awake. . . .*

Nervously she peeped round the curtain again. Merriman and Will strode to the centre of the quay. A third figure, cloaked and hooded, joined them from the other side of the harbour. Standing very tall, facing the village and the hills, Merriman raised both arms in the air. And although nothing could be seen, it was as though a great wave of rage came roaring at them, rearing over them, out of the dark haunted village of Trewissick.

Jane could stand no more of it. With an unhappy little moan she dived across the room and into her bed. Tight over her head she pulled the covers, and lay there stuffy and shivering. She was not afraid for her own safety; Merriman had promised her that the cottage was protected, and she believed him. Nor was she afraid for those figures down in the harbour; if they had survived so strange a succession of monstrosities, they could survive anything. In any case nothing could harm Merriman. It was another fear that possessed Jane: a dreadful horror of the unknown, of whatever force was sweeping through land and sea, out there. She wanted only to cower into her own corner, animal-like, away from it, safe.

So this she did, and found, oddly, that because the fear was so large and formless, it proved more ready to go away.

Gradually Jane stopped shivering; grew warm. Her taut limbs relaxed; she began to breathe slowly and deeply. And then she slept.

CHAPTER ELEVEN

DOWN IN THE HARBOUR WITH WILL AND CAPTAIN TOMS AT either side, shadowy hooded figures, Merriman raised both arms higher in a gesture that was half-appeal, half-command, and he called into the darkness over Trewissick in his deep resonant voice the words of the spell of Mana and the spell of Reck and the spell of Lir.

From all around, rage beat at them like waves, a great gale of unseen force.

"No!" cried the great voice of the Greenwitch, thick with fury. "No! Leave me alone!"

"Come forth, Greenwitch!" Merriman called. "The spells command it."

"One coming is all they may command," the voice roared. "And out of the sea I came, they commanded me and I came. No more, no more!"

"Come forth, Greenwitch!" Will's clear voice sang out through the darkness like a beam of light. "The White Lady bids you hear us. Tethys gave us leave to call you, before you should go to the deep."

Fury enveloped them like a tidal wave. At their backs, the

sea growled and murmured; the land quivered beneath their feet.

But then, though they could not see it, the presence was all around them, seething, resentful.

Merriman said: "The secret is not yours, Greenwitch. You know you should not keep it."

"I found it. It was in the sea."

"It would not have been there, but for a battle between the Light and the Dark. It fell, it was lost."

"It was in the sea, in my mother's realm."

"Come, my friend," Captain Toms said gently, in his rounded Cornish voice. "You know that it is not of the sea, but is a part of a Thing of Power."

The Greenwitch said, "I have no friend. It matters nothing to me what happens between the Light and the Dark."

"Ah," Merriman said. "You will find out that it may matter, if this Thing of Power shall belong fully to the Dark. Half of it they have already, half they seek to have from you. If they gain it, and have the power of the whole, things will go hard with the world of men."

The voice around them mumbled, "Men have nothing to do with—"

"Men have nothing to do with me?" Will's voice cut light and clear through the night. "Do you believe that, Greenwitch? Men have everything to do with you. Without them, you would not exist. They make you, each year. Each year, they throw you to the sea. Without men, the Greenwitch would never have been born."

"They do not make *me*." The great voice was bitter. "They serve themselves only, their own needs only. Though they make me in the form of a creature, yet they are making no more than an offering, as once in older days it might have been a slaughtered cock, or sheep, or man. I am an offering, Old

Ones, no more. If they thought I had life they would kill me as they killed the cocks and the sheep and the men, to make a sacrifice. Instead they make me as an image, out of branches and leaves. It is a game, a substitute. I am given real life only by the White Lady, life enough to take me down to the deeps. And this once too I have had a different life wake in me, because I was drawn out to the earth, out of the sea, by. . . ." the voice grew reflective; a note of cunning crept in . . . "by the Dark."

"Put that out of your mind," Merriman said at once. "None is more self-serving than the Dark. Tethys has told you that."

"Self-serving!" The bitterness was back in an instant, and far deeper. "You are all self-servers, Light, Dark, men. There is no place for the Wild Magic except its own . . . no care . . . no care. . . ."

In spite of themselves the three Old Ones swayed backwards as the force of fury rose again abruptly, and the rage of the Greenwitch throbbed all around them like a great heart fiercely beating.

Staggering, Merriman caught himself upright, sweeping his long cloak around him, the hood falling back to leave his wild white hair glistening in the lamplight. "Has no-one showed care for you, Greenwitch? No-one?"

"No-one!" The huge voice rang through the village, around the hills, over the moors behind; like distant thunder it rumbled and re-echoed. "No creature! None! Not . . . one. . . ." The fierceness died, the thunder grew less. For a long moment they were listening only to the wash of the uneasy sea against the cliffs, out where the swells broke. Then the Greenwitch said in a whisper, "None except one. None except the child."

"The child?" Will said involuntarily. A thin note of raw incredulity tipped his voice; for a moment he thought the Greenwitch meant himself.

Merriman said softly, ignoring him, "The child who wished you well."

"She was up at the headland at the making," the Greenwitch said. "And they told her of the old saying, that whoever touches the Greenwitch before it be put to cliff, and makes a wish, shall have that wish. So then she could have made any wish she chose." The voice grew warm, for the first time. "She could have wished for anything, Old Ones, even for the first lost part of your Thing of Power to come back to you. Yet when she touched me she looked at me as if I were human, and she said, 'I wish you could be happy.' "

The soft thunder died away; the harbour was silent, bursting with the memory that filled it.

"*I wish you could be happy*," the Greenwitch said softly.

"So she—" Will began; but stopped, as Merriman's hand touched his arm. The air around them was growing bright, light, mild; Trewissick, for this one night, would catch every mood of the Greenwitch like a burning-glass. The echoing voice murmured softly to itself, and it seemed to Will that with every moment the earth and sea in that place grew gentler.

Into the dim-lit spring night a cold voice said, "The girl too is self-serving, just as the rest of them."

There was a silence. Then out of the shadows at the back of the quay stepped the painter, the man of the Dark. He stood in a pool of yellow lamplight, facing them, a chunky black silhouette.

"Self-serving," he said to the air. "Self-serving." Then turning to Merriman he said, "I have the mastery of it, not you. The spells that called it from the ocean were mine. The creature is mine to command, Old One, not yours."

Will felt a low rumbling around them, and saw the lights faintly quiver.

Merriman said, "This is not now a matter for command,

but for gentleness. The spells that brought it out of the sea can accomplish no more now."

The painter laughed scornfully. He swung round in a half-circle, arms outstretched. "Greenwitch!" he shouted. "I have come back for the secret. I give you one last chance, before the wrath of the Dark will descend!"

The rumbling sound rose into a huge snarl, like a roll of thunder, then died down again.

"Be careful," said Captain Toms softly. "Be very careful."

But the command in the voice of the man of the Dark now was like ice; it was the cold absolute arrogance that through centuries past had brought men down to terror and grovelling obedience. "Greenwitch!" the man called into the night. "Give your secret to the Dark! Obey! The Dark is come again, and for the last time, Greenwitch! The hour is come!"

Will clenched his fists so that the nails cut into his palms; even an Old One could feel the force of such a command bite into the mind. He watched without a breath, wondering; he did not know how such a challenge would touch the Wild Magic, a force neither of the Light nor of the Dark nor of men.

The air around them sang with the ferocity of the Dark messenger's will, spinning their wits into uncertainty—and then gradually, subtly, a change began. The force that was in the air faltered, and changed imperceptibly back to the spell-web that had possessed this small part of the earth since the Greenwitch had struck the painter down. The Wild Magic was resisting all challenge, invincible as the Boar Trwyth. Will took a great breath; he began to guess what was to come.

Standing alone on the quay, the painter whirled round, staggering, groping into the air, as if in search for something he could not see. Out of the darkness, high above the village, a weird clear voice called, as it had called before:

The hour is come, but not the man.
The hour is come, but not the man.
The hour is come, but not the man.

And into the silence after the ringing words a whispering began, a gradual murmuring of many voices, calling, whispering: *Roger Toms! Roger Toms!* And shadows came flocking into the harbour, from all sides, all the shades and spirits and hauntings of that one haunted night: the past folk of Trewissick from all the centuries that the little sea-town had ever seen, focused into one black point of time. *Roger Toms! Roger Toms!* they called, softly at first, growing gradually louder, louder. It was a calling and an accusing and a judgement, and it whispered relentlessly round the harbour and over the sea.

Silently, unobtrusively, the three Old Ones drew their hoods over their heads and moved together to one side of the harbour, in the shade of the wall, to stand there unseen.

Out in the centre of the quay, alone, the dark painter turned in a slow circle, incredulously seeing and hearing the past come falling upon him, making him into its long shame. With immense effort he raised his arms, pushing feebly at the air.

But there was no pushing away the unreasoning rage that the Wild Magic had brought out of the village, to make a scapegoat of its attacker. "*Roger Toms! Roger Toms!*" the voices called angrily, stronger, more demanding.

The painter shrieked into the night, "I am not he! You mistake me!"

"Roger Toms!" came a great triumphant shout.

"No! No!"

They were all around him, crying and calling, pointing, just as the villagers of the present had crowded and called and pushed about the Greenwitch, as it was taken newly-made to tumble headlong from the cliff.

And from out of the night, over the roofs of Trewissick from the dark inland moors, came sailing again the phantom ship of Cornwall, single-masted, square-rigged, with a dinghy behind, that had sailed up out of the midnight sea in the haunting. Silently it skimmed over houses and roads and quayside, and this time it was not empty, but had a figure at the helm. The drowned man, dripping and intent, whom Jane had seen glide up out of the sea, stood high on the deck at the wheel, steering his black dead vessel, looking neither to left nor right. And with a glad shriek all the great crowd of shades rushed on to the ship, dragging with them the struggling painter.

"*Roger Toms! Roger Toms!*"

"No!"

The phantom sails filled again with a wind that no man alive could feel, and the ship sailed away, out to sea, out into the night, and on Trewissick quay the Old Ones were left alone.

*   *   *

Jane slept deeply at first, but halfway through the night dreams began to edge into her sleep. She saw the painter, painting; she saw again all the fearful things that she had seen from her window that night. She dreamed of Roger Toms and the fair-traders, with the ship called the *Lottery* fleeing from the Revenue men and the shots ringing out between the two; and in her dream the *Lottery* became the black phantom ship that had sailed unthinkably up out of the sea and away across the land.

She thought, as she tossed in her sleep, that she heard voices calling *Roger Toms! Roger Toms!* And then as they faded, gradually into her dream came the Greenwitch. She could not see it, as she had seen it in a dream once before; this time it was obscure, merely a voice, lost in the shadows. It was unhappy. *Poor thing*, Jane thought, *it's always unhappy.*

She said, "Greenwitch, what are all these horrible things?"

"It is the Wild Magic," the Greenwitch said miserably into her dreaming mind. "This is how it besets the minds of men, calling up all the terrors they have ever had, or their forefathers have ever had. All the old hauntings of Cornwall, which men there have always feared, that is what these have been."

"But why tonight?" Jane said.

The Greenwitch sighed, a great gusty sigh like the sea. "Because I was angry. I am never angry, but the man of the Dark made me so. And the rage of those who are part of the Wild Magic is not a good thing to bring out. The village bore it, the village has been possessed. . . ."

"Is it over now?"

"It is over now." The Greenwitch sighed again. "The Wild Magic has carried away the man of the Dark. The messenger of the Dark. He was a creature alone, trying to cheat his masters. So they did not protect him, and so the Wild Magic has taken him to outer Time, from which he may never properly come back. . . ."

Jane cried, "But he has the grail! What about the grail?"

"I know nothing of a grail," the Greenwitch said indifferently. "What is a grail?"

"It doesn't matter," Jane said, with effort. "Did he take your secret, in the end? Did you give it him?"

"It is mine," the Greenwitch said quickly. "I found it. And now no-one will let me keep it."

"Did you give it to the Dark?"

"No,"

"Thank goodness," Jane said. "It really is terribly important, Greenwitch. To the Light, to everyone. Really. To the people who made you, to my brothers and me, to all of us."

The Greenwitch said, "To you?" Its great melancholy voice echoed round her like waves booming in a cave. "My secret is important to you?"

"Of course it is," said Jane.

"Then here," said the huge voice. "Take it."

Jane never knew afterwards what she had been at that moment doing in her dream: standing or sitting or lying, indoors or out, in day or night, under sea or over stone. She remembered only the great wave of astonished delight. "Greenwitch! You will give me your secret?"

"Here," said the voice again, and there in Jane's hand was the small misshapen lead case, that had fallen into the sea at the end of the adventure that had achieved the grail—and that held inside it the only manuscript able to unravel for them the secret of the grail. "Take it," the Greenwitch said. "You made a wish that was for me, not for yourself. No-one has ever done that. I give you my secret, in return."

"Thank you," said Jane, in a whisper. All around her was darkness; it was as though nothing existed in the whole world but herself, standing in emptiness, and the great disembodied voice of this strange wild thing, a creature of the sea made of branches and leaves from the earth. "Thank you, Greenwitch. I shall find you a better secret, instead." A quick image came flashing into her mind. "I shall put it in the same place where you found this one."

"Too late," said the great sad voice. "Too late. . . ." It boomed and re-echoed, fading gradually away. "I go to my mother now, to the great deeps." Away into the darkness the echoes died, a last whisper lingering. "Too late . . . too late. . . ."

"Greenwitch!" Jane cried in distress. "Come back! Come back!" She ran blindly into the darkness, reaching out helplessly. "Come back!"

And in the same moment, the dream dissolved, and she woke.

She woke into the small white room bright with sunshine, gay as the cheerful yellow curtains at the windows, and the yellow quilt pulled up to her chin on the bed. The curtains shifted gently in a small breeze from the window she had left part-open the night before.

And clenched in Jane's hand was a small misshapen lead case, patched with green stains, like a rock that has been a long time under the sea.

CHAPTER TWELVE

TOUSLE-HEADED FROM SLEEP, RUMPLED PYJAMAS FLAPPING, THE children rushed unceremoniously into Merriman's bedroom.

"Where is he?"

"Try downstairs. Come on!"

Merriman and Will, looking as though they had been up and dressed for hours, were calmly eating their breakfast in the long low living-room. As Simon, Jane and Barney tumbled into the room Merriman lowered a large rustling stretch of newspaper, and peered at them over a pair of gold-rimmed half-spectacles perched startlingly on his high-arched nose.

He said, looking at the battered leaden cylinder that Jane mutely held out to him, "Ah."

Will put down his toast, grinning all over his round face. "Well done, Jane," he said.

Jane said, "But I didn't do anything. It just—it just appeared."

"You made a wish," said Will.

She stared at him.

"Aren't we going to open it?" Barney said impatiently. "Come on, Gumerry."

"Well," Merriman said. He took the small lead case from

Jane's hand and set it on the table, dark eyes glittering in his deep-lined face. "Well now."

Jane was still staring, her gaze flickering between Will and her great-uncle. "You knew I had it. You knew."

"We hoped," Merriman said gently.

Simon put a finger on the case as if he were saying a prayer. "It's been in the sea so long. Look at it, there's weed and stuff all over it . . . won't the water have got in? That would be my fault, from last summer. I opened it just once, to see what was inside, and then closed it again. Imagine if the manuscript's all ruined in there, if I didn't close it tightly enough . . ."

"Stop it," said Jane.

Merriman took up the case in his long wiry fingers, and gently he tugged and turned the green-splashed grey metal until suddenly one end of it came away in his hand like a cap. Inside, a small roll of heavy parchment projected from the longer part of the case like a pointing finger.

"It's all right!" Simon said hoarsely. Hastily he cleared his throat and put his shoulders back, though it was hard to recover dignity in pyjamas.

Barney hugged himself, jiggling with impatience. "What does it say? What does it say?"

Very slowly, and with immense care, Merriman drew the rolled manuscript from the little leaden case. He said, as he unrolled it gently on the table, flat under one large hand, "We shall be able to do this twice, at the most, unless it is to crumble into dust. So this is the first time."

His long fingers held the cracking brown parchment open on the white cloth. It was covered with two blocks of heavy black marks. The children stared, dismay chasing horror over their faces.

"But it doesn't say anything! That's not even a language!"

"It's gibberish!"

Jane said slowly, more cautious, "What is the writing, Gumerry? *Is* there any kind of alphabet like that?"

She looked without hope at the series of black marks: upright strokes, slanting strokes, single and in groups, like the random doodling of a tidy madman.

"Yes," Merriman said. "There is." He lifted his hand so that the manuscript rolled itself again, and Will, who had been looking over his shoulder, went quietly back to his chair. "There is an ancient alphabet called Ogham, not intended for our kind of writing—this is something like that. But still it is a half-writing, a cipher. Remember, it cannot mean anything until we have the grail—it was written to go with the inscription on the grail, to show its meaning plain. The one will give light to the other."

Barney wailed, "But we haven't got the grail!"

"The Dark," Simon said bitterly. "The painter." Then he stiffened, his face full of wild hope. "But we can get it, we can go and take it from his caravan. They took him to—"

"Morning! Morning!" Mrs Penhallow came bustling in with a tray. "I heard your voices, m'dears, so here's your breakfasts."

"Super!" said Barney at once.

Very gently, Merriman let his newspaper droop over the manuscript and its case.

"Well," Jane said, pulling helplessly at her rumpled dressing-gown. "We aren't exactly dressed, but thank you."

"My goodness, who minds about that, on holiday? Now you just help yourselves and relax, and I'll use the time to do your rooms." Leaving the tray, she bounced out into the kitchen; then reappeared with broom and dusters. When she was safely creaking away up the stairs behind the cottages' connecting door, Simon let out a long breath and burst out again, taut and excited.

"They took him to hospital, so we can go to the caravan, he won't be there! He—"

Will hissed sharply between his teeth, holding up a hand in warning. A stumbling and mumbling came at the other door into the room, and through it appeared Bill Stanton, yawning, blinking, tying the belt of an improbable dressing-gown striped like a deck-chair. He looked at the Drews, covering the last of his yawns. "Well," he said. "I'm glad someone at least looks the same way I do."

Simon sat down hard in his chair and began fiercely slicing bread.

Barney said, "Did you get on all right last night, Mr Stanton?"

Will's uncle groaned. "Don't talk about it. What an evening! That crazy guy we were taking to hospital ran away."

"Ran away?" The room was suddenly very quiet.

Mr Stanton sat down and reached greedily for the teapot. "I hope he's all right," he said. "But he sure gave us enough trouble. He was as quiet as anything there in the back seat, I'd have sworn he was still out like a light. Never made a sound. Then when we were about halfway to St Austell, very bleak part of the road, something ran out in front of the car, and I hit it." He took a long drink of tea, and sighed gratefully. "So I stopped, and hopped out to take a look. I mean, you don't want to leave an animal in pain, do you? And while I was out there in the dark, this fellow in the back seat jumped up and opened the door on the other side, and was off out over the fields before Frannie knew what was happening."

"But he was hurt," Jane said. "Could he run?"

"Ran like a hare," Mr Stanton said, pushing back the hair wisping over his bald head. "We could hear him crashing about, through hedges I suppose. We looked for him for quite a while, but we didn't have a light and it's none too friendly out there in bad weather in the dark. So in the end we drove on to St Austell and told the police what had happened.

Fran thought we should, after getting Captain Toms to tell the Trewissick cop. Though it turned out in the end he didn't, eh, Merry?"

"We tried," Merriman said blandly. "P.C. Tregear was out of the village."

"Well, the St Austell constabulary thought we were nuts," said Mr Stanton, "and they were probably right. In the end we came back here. Very late." He drank some more tea, and sighed again. "English-born though I am," he said plaintively, "I do wish our good Mrs Penhallow would make coffee for breakfast now and again."

"What was the animal you hit?" Barney said.

"We never found a sign of it. I suppose it was a cat. It looked bigger—might have been a badger perhaps. By the time we were through"— he chuckled— "we'd decided it was just a good old Cornish ghost."

"Oh," Jane said faintly.

"Well, enough of that," Mr Stanton said. "We all did our Good Samaritan bit, and I presume the guy's all right somewhere. Hey, this is your last day, kids, isn't it? Looks like it's going to be a nice one. Frannie was wondering if we could all take a picnic on to that big beach the other side of Kemare Head."

"That sounds delightful," Merriman said swiftly, before they could react. "A little later this morning, hmmm? There's one thing I want to show them all first."

"That's fine. It's going to take me a while to recover from last night. I don't think Fran's even awake yet."

"What do you want to show us, Gumerry?" said Jane, more from politeness than enthusiasm.

"Oh," Merriman said. "Just an old farm."

*　　*　　*

They bounced through the village in Merriman's big car: Jane and Captain Toms in front, the boys behind, with a happy, fidgeting Rufus. All the windows were open; with no wind, and the sun rising high already, it promised to be an uncommonly hot spring day.

Simon said, "But he'll be there waiting for us! He's bound to be, that's why he ran away! Gumerry, how can we possibly just drive up in a car?"

A note of frantic worry was rising in his voice; Will looked at him with sympathy, but said nothing.

Merriman said at last, without turning his head, "The man of the Dark will not trouble us again, Simon."

Barney said, "Why not?"

Simon said, "How do you know?"

"He tried once more, once too often, to challenge the rights of the Greenwitch," Merriman said, swinging the car round a corner. "And the Wild Magic, to which the Greenwitch belongs, carried him away." He fell silent, in the kind of silence that they knew meant an end of questioning.

"Last night," said Simon.

"Yes," Merriman said. Jane, glancing sideways at his eagle-bleak profile, wondered for a cold moment what exactly had happened to the painter of the Dark, and then, remembering what she had seen, was glad that she did not know.

And before they realised they had gone so far, the big car was turning off the road on to a narrow side-lane, roofed by low-branching trees, past a notice that read: PENTREATH FARM.

Simon said nervously, "Shouldn't we walk?"

Wilfully misunderstanding, Merriman waved one hand airily. "Oh no, don't worry, this old bus has stood a lot worse bumps than this in her time."

Simon tried to swallow his uneasiness. He stared out of the window at the green banks of grass and the thick-swelling trees; at the lacy branches brushing the windows. Unconsciously he clenched his hands together as they approached the last turn in the lane before they would see the painter's caravan, and at the last swing of the car tightened his grip and fought the impulse to close his eyes.

And squinting unhappily out at the green bush-scattered field, he saw that the caravan was not there.

"Stop a moment," he said, in a high unfamiliar voice. Merriman stopped the car without question, and Simon tumbled out, with Barney close behind him. Together they hurried to the spot where, they both knew very well, the glittering Gipsy caravan had stood; where the horse had moved lazily cropping the grass; where the man of the Dark had used Barney's mind for his own ends. There was no sign that anything or anyone had been there for months. Not a blade of grass was bent, not a branch flattened. Rufus, who had jumped out of the car after them, moved restlessly over the ground with his nose down, casting about in circles, finding no scent. Then he paused; lifted his head, shook it from side to side in a strange undog-like manner, like someone with a ringing in his ears, and made off at a swift trot round the next corner in the road.

"Rufus!" Simon shouted. "Rufus!"

"Let him be," said Captain Toms clearly from the car. "Come back here, and we shall follow him."

On down the lane the big car purred, and then they were round the last corner and facing the farm.

The low grey building seemed even more decrepit than Simon had remembered. He looked with more attention now at the beams of wood nailed cross-shaped over the front door; at the new growth of creeper reaching over windows unhindered; at other windows, here and there, black and broken like missing teeth. Long grass rose lush and new round rusting pieces of farm equipment left in the yard: a skeletal old plough, a harrow, the remains of a tractor with its great tyres gone. In the pen of a deserted pig-sty, nettles grew tall and rank. Somewhere behind the farmhouse, Rufus barked shrilly, and a flurry of pigeons flapped into the air. There was a wet smell of growing things.

Captain Toms said softly, "The wild is taking Pentreath Farm, very fast."

Merriman stood in the middle of the farmyard, looking about him, perplexed. The lines in his face seemed deeper-carved than before. Captain Toms leaned against the car, gazing at the farm, one hand absently tracing patterns in the damp earth with his stick.

Will peered in through one of the front windows of the farm, straining to see through the murk. "I suppose we should go inside," he said, without much conviction.

"I don't think so," Simon said. He stood at Will's shoulder, and for once there was no tension between them, but only the studying of a common problem. "Somehow I'm sure the painter never went in there. It looked absolutely untouched last time. He seemed just to be living in the caravan on his own. He was a separate sort of man."

"Separate indeed." Merriman's deep voice came to them across the yard. "A strange creature of the Dark, that they sent out as a thief only, to take the grail and hide it. It was a good moment to choose, for we were off our guard, thinking them too preoccupied with licking their wounds after a great defeat. . . . But the creature of the Dark was willing to betray his masters, having greater ideas. He knew the tale of the lost manuscript, and he thought that if he could secretly get that for himself as well, and thus complete one of the Things of Power, he could by a sort of blackmail make himself one of the great lords of the Dark."

Jane said, "But didn't they know what he was doing?"

"They were not expecting him to over-reach his commission,"

Merriman said. "They knew, better perhaps than he did himself, how hopeless a fate lay waiting any lone figure who might venture on such a quest. We think they were not watching him, but simply waiting for his return."

"The Dark is indeed preoccupied, for a time," Captain Toms said. "They have damage to repair, from certain happenings midwinter last. They will make little showing of themselves, until the time of their next great rising."

Simon said slowly, "Perhaps that's what the painter meant when he said to Barney, *Am I observed?* Do you remember? I thought he was talking about you, but he must have meant his own masters."

"Where is Barney?" Will said, looking round.

"Barney? Hey, Barney!"

An unintelligible shout came from somewhere beyond the far side of the farmhouse.

"Oh dear," said Jane. "Now what's he up to?"

They ran in the direction of the shout, Merriman following more slowly with Captain Toms. A great rambling tangle of weeds and nettles and brambles rose at the side of the old house, and all around the outbuildings beyond.

"Ow!" Barney howled from somewhere inside the thicket. "I'm stung!"

"What on earth are you doing?"

"Looking for Rufus."

They heard a muffled barking; it seemed to come from the further of the two outbuildings, an old stone barn with a perilous half-fallen roof.

"Ow!" Barney yelped again. "Mind the nettles, they're fierce. . . . Rufus just goes on barking and doesn't come out, I think he must be stuck. He went this way. . . ."

Captain Toms limped forward. "Rufus!" he called, very loud and stern. "Here! Come here!"

There was more muffled excited barking from the ramshackle barn, ending in a snuffling whine.

Captain Toms sighed, and pulled his grey beard. "Foolish beast," he said. "Stand clear a minute. Look out, Barney." Sweeping his heavy walking-stick from side to side as if it were a scythe, he moved gradually forwards, thrashing a path through the nettles and undergrowth to the crumbling stone sides of the barn. Rufus' barking, inside, became more frenzied still.

"Shut up, dog," called Barney, at the captain's elbow now. "We're coming!" He wriggled round to a rotting wooden door, hanging sideways from one hinge, and peered in through the V-shaped gap between door and wall. "He must have got in here and knocked something over that blocked the gap. . . . I can get in here, if I. . . ."

"Do be careful," Jane said.

" 'Course," said Barney. He squeezed in round the tilted door, pushing aside something that fell with a crumbling clatter, and disappeared. There was a burst of joyful barking inside the barn, and then Rufus came leaping out through the gap, tongue lolling, tail waving. He pranced up to Captain Toms. He was very dirty; small damp pieces of rotten wood speckled his red coat, and cobwebs clung stickily round his nose.

Captain Toms patted him absent-mindedly. He was looking at the barn, with a faint puzzled frown on his face. Then he glanced questioningly at Merriman; following his gaze, Jane saw the same look in her great-uncle's eyes. What was the matter with them? Before she could ask, Barney's head poked out of the gap in the barn door. His hair was dishevelled and one cheek was smeared grey, but Jane's attention was caught only by the unsmiling blankness of his face. He looked as though he had had a very bad shock.

"Come out of there, Barney," Merriman said. "That roof's not safe."

Barney said, "I'm just coming. But please, Gumerry, could Simon come in here just for a minute first? It's important."

Merriman glanced from Captain Toms to Will and back to Barney. His stern-lined face was tense. "All right. For a moment."

Simon slipped past them to wriggle his way through the gap. Behind him Will said diffidently, "Would you mind if I came too?"

Jane winced, waiting for the inevitable snub; but Simon only said briefly, "Fine. Come on."

The two boys wriggled in after Barney. Simon flinched as a splintered edge scraped his arm; the gap was narrower than it looked. Scrambling to his feet, he stood coughing as Will came in after him. The dust was thick on the floor, and it was hard at first to see clearly in the half-light from dirty, overgrown windows.

Blinking, Simon saw Barney beckoning him.

"Over here. Look."

He followed Barney to one end of the barn, clear of the piled timber and logs that filled much of the floor. And then he stopped.

Before him, ghostly in the shadows of corner and roof, stood a Gipsy caravan, of exactly the same shape and pattern as the one in which they had met the painter of the Dark. There were the tall outward-sloping sides, the insets of carved wood beneath the eaves of the overhanging wooden roof. There, at the far end, were the shafts for the horse, and at this end the divided door—in two halves, swinging, like a stable door—reached by a wooden stairway-ladder of six steps. And the top step was the step on which, at the end, they had stood. . . .

But of course it could not be the same. This caravan was not shiny-neat, or newly painted. This caravan had dusty worn sides in which only odd patches of ancient paint remained, flaking away. This caravan had one broken shaft, and the top half of its split door hung from half a hinge. It was old and beaten, unused, unloved; the glass in its windows was long broken. It could not have been moved from its place for the many years since the roof of the old barn had begun to sag, for at the further end of the barn the roof-beams lay rotted with all their remaining weight resting on top of the caravan.

It was a relic, an antique. Simon stared. It was as if he were meeting the great-great-grandfather of a boy he knew well, and finding that the old man had exactly the same face as the boy, but immensely, impossibly aged.

He opened his mouth and looked at Barney, but could think of nothing to say.

Barney said flatly, "It must have been here for years and years and years. Since long before we were born."

Will said, "How well do you remember the inside of the painter's caravan?"

Simon and Barney both jumped at the sound of his voice; they had forgotten he was there. Now they turned; Will stood near the door of the barn, half-hidden in shadow, only his amiable blank face blinking at them in clear light.

Barney said, "Fairly well."

"And you, Simon?" Will said. Without leaving time for an answer, he went on, "Barney doesn't remember seeing the grail at all. But you remember everything, from the moment when he first took out the box it was in."

"Yes," Simon said. With a vague, detached interest, he realised that for the first time he was listening to Will as though he were older, without resentment or argument.

Will said nothing more. He crossed from behind them to the steps at the end of the old caravan, pushing aside with his toe the dust and debris that lay cluttered everywhere. He went up the steps. He took hold of the top loose-hanging half of the caravan door, and it came away in his hands, as the rust-eaten hinge crumbled into dust. Then he tugged sharply at the bottom half of the door, and it swung reluctantly towards him with the slow creak of an old farm gate.

"Barney," he said. "Do you mind going inside?"

" 'Course not," Barney said boldly, but his steps towards the caravan door were reluctant and slow.

Simon said nothing to help him. He was looking at Will, whose voice, as once before, had a crispness and certainty that raised inexplicable echoes in his head.

"Simon," Will said. "What did the painter say, word for word, when he first directed Barney to the place where he found the grail?"

Half-closing his eyes, concentrating fiercely, Simon pushed his mind backwards and looked to see what was in it. "We were both about halfway inside," he said. Like a sleep-walker he went forwards up the ricketty old steps, his hand on Barney's shoulder gently propelling him, and with Will following, the two of them walked into the little room that made the inside of the van.

"And the man said, because Barney had said he was thirsty, *'In that cupboard by your right foot you will find some cans of orange soda. And . . . and you might bring out a cardboard box you'll find in there too.'* So Barney did that."

Barney turned his head and looked nervously at Will, and the Will who was somehow not quite Will beamed encouragingly, as if he were after all no more than the amiable foolish-looking boy they had met at the beginning of this small strange holiday. So Barney looked down at his right foot, and saw beside it a low cupboard with no handle and the clutter of years mounded against its door; and he crouched on his knees and cleared away the rubbish and scrabbled with his fingernails to find enough leverage to open the small door. When at last it swung open, he felt inside and brought out a battered, damp, evil-smelling cardboard box.

He set it on the floor. All three of them stared at it in silence. Faintly from outside the barn they heard Jane's light voice cry anxiously, "Are you all right? Hey, do come on out!"

Will said softly, "Open it."

Slowly, reluctantly, Barney took hold of the top of the box. The ancient rotting cardboard came away in his hand, and a brightness was in their eyes, a golden radiance that seemed to fill the decrepit, crumbling remnants of what had once a long time ago been a caravan. And there shining beneath their eyes was the grail.

CHAPTER THIRTEEN

IN THE FARMYARD, IN FRONT OF THE HOUSE, A GREAT ROUND piece of granite was set into the ground: an old mill-wheel, worn and grass-fringed. On its bright-flecked grey surface they set the grail, and gathered round as Merriman took from his pocket the battered little cylinder that held the manuscript. He slid out the small roll of parchment, its edges cracked and flaking, and unrolled it to lie on the uneven stone.

"And this is the second time for looking," he said.

The children picked up stones from the grass and laid them gently on the edges to hold the parchment flat. Then instinctively they drew to one side, to let Merriman and Captain Toms study the grail and manuscript together.

Barney, next to Merriman, suddenly realised that Will was standing quiet and unmoving behind him. He ducked quickly aside. "Here," he said. "Come on."

The golden grail glittered in the sunlight; the engraving on its sides was clear and clean, but the smooth beaten gold of the inside surface, as Simon had said, was blackened and dark. Will looked now at the close, delicate engraving for the first time in his life, seeing the panels filled with vivid scenes of men running, fighting, crouching behind shields: tunic-clad, strangely-helmeted men brandishing swords and shields. The pictures woke deep memories in him of things he had forgotten he had ever known. He looked closer, at the words and letters interwoven between the figures, and at the last panel on the grail, completely filled with words in this same cipher-language that no living scholar had been able to understand. And like the other two Old Ones, he began methodically to look from the marks on the old manuscript to the marks on the grail, and gradually the interweaving became clear.

Will found himself breathing faster, as the meaning of the inscription began to take shape in his mind.

Staring at the manuscript, Merriman said slowly, painfully, as if he were spelling out a hard lesson:

> On the day of the dead, when the year too dies,
> Must the youngest open the oldest hills
> Through the door of the birds, where the breeze breaks.
> There fire shall fly from the raven boy,
> And the silver eyes that see the wind,
> And the Light shall have the harp of gold.

He stopped, his face tight with concentration. "Not easy," he said to himself. "The pattern is hard to keep."

Captain Toms leaned on his heavy stick, peering at another panel of the grail. He said softly, his accent cradling the words:

> By the pleasant lake the Sleepers lie,
> On Cadfan's Way where the kestrels call;
> Though grim from the Grey King shadows fall,
> Yet singing the golden harp shall guide
> To break their sleep and bid them ride.

Will knelt down beside the granite slab and turned the grail again. Slowly he read aloud:

When light from the lost land shall return,
Six Sleepers shall ride, six Signs shall burn,
And where the midsummer tree grows tall
By Pendragon's sword the Dark shall fall.

Merriman stood upright. "And the last line of all will be the spell," he said, looking hard at Will; the deep-set dark eyes bored into his mind. "Remember. *Y maent yr mynyddoedd yn canu, ac y mae'r arglwyddes yn dod.* The mountains are singing, and the Lady comes. Remember."

He leaned down to the rock, moved aside the stone weights and took up the small curling manuscript in one big hand. As if the Drews did not exist at all, he looked down at Will and Captain Toms.

"You have it all?" he said.

"Yes," said Will.

"Safe remembered," Captain Toms said.

In one sharp movement Merriman clenched his fist, and the little roll of stiff, broken-edged parchment crumbled instantly into tiny fragments, small as gravel, light as dust. He opened his long fingers and swung his arm wide, and in a dusty shower the pieces flew away in every direction, into oblivion.

The children cried out sharply.

"Gumerry!" Jane stared at him, appalled. "You've ruined the whole thing!"

"No," Merriman said.

"But you can't understand what the grail says, without it, No-one can." Simon's face was creased with perplexity. "It'll be just as much of a mystery as it was before!"

"Not to us," Captain Toms said. He eased himself down to sit on the granite slab, and took up the grail, turning it in his fingers so that the sunlight glinted on the engraved sides. "We know, now, what is in the hidden message of the grail. It will shape the next twelve months of our lives, and help us to save men from great terror, very soon, for all time. And now that we have it in our minds, we shall never forget."

"I've forgotten it already," Barney said plaintively. "Everything except a bit about a golden harp, and a grey king. How can you have a grey king?"

"Of course you have forgotten it," Captain Toms said. "That was the intention." He smiled at Barney. "And we do not even need an enchantment to help you forget, as our friend from the Dark did. We can rely on the mortality of your memory."

"And you don't have to worry about whether anyone else will remember," Simon said, slowly understanding, "because no-one else will ever hear or see."

Jane said sadly, "It seems a pity that the poor Greenwitch's secret should just be thrown away."

"It has served its purpose," Merriman said. His deep voice rose a little, gained a hint of ceremony. "Its high purpose, for which it was made so very long ago. It has set us the next great step along the road to keep the Dark from rising, and there is nothing more important than that quest."

"That last bit you said, from the grail and the manuscript," Barney said. "What language was it in?"

"Welsh," Merriman said.

"Is the last part of the quest in Wales?"

"Yes."

"Are we going to be part of it?"

Merriman said, "Wait and see."

*   *   *

They lay in variously abandoned attitudes in the sunshine on the beach, recovering from an enormous picnic lunch. Simon and Barney were lazily tossing a ball to and fro, without bothering to stand up. Bill Stanton was eying them, and the nearby cricket bat, with nostalgic optimism.

"Just wait," he said to his sun-bathing wife, "we'll show you just exactly how it's played, in a little while."

"Great," said Fran Stanton sleepily.

Jane, lying on her back blinking up at the blue sky, propped herself up on her elbows and looked out to sea. The sand was hot against her skin; it was a beautiful, sunny, breezeless Cornish day, of a rare and special kind.

"I'm just going for a little walk," she said to nobody in particular, and over the dry sand she went, across the long golden beach, towards the rocks that glistened with low-tide seaweed at the foot of Kemare Head. The headland reared up above her, grassy slope changing to jagged grey cliff; at the very tip, the cliffs towered in a sheer wall against the sky. Jane's head was full of memories. She began to walk over the rocks, wincing a little as her bare feet, not yet toughened by summer, pressed against rough rock. Out here, last year, she and Barney and Simon had reached the peak of their adventure, the achieving of the grail that had lain for hundreds of years in a cave, the entrance covered totally by water at all but the lowest tides. Out here, they had fled from the pursuing Dark, with the grail and the little lead case they had found inside it. And out here, she thought as she reached the furthest point of the rocks, with the waves breaking white at her feet, just here, in the flurry of saving the grail, the little lead case had plummeted into the waves and down to the bottom of the sea.

And the Greenwitch had found it there, and made it a precious secret.

Jane looked at the deep green water beyond the breaking waves. "Good-by, Greenwitch," she said softly.

She unclasped a small silver bracelet that she wore on her

wrist, weighed it experimentally in her hand, and drew back her arm to throw it into the sea.

A voice said gently behind her, "Don't do that."

Jane gasped, and nearly lost her balance; swinging round, she saw Will Stanton.

"Oh!" she said. "You made me jump."

"Sorry," Will said. He balanced his way forwards to stand beside her; his bare feet looked very white against the dark seaweed patching the rocks.

Jane looked at his pleasant round face, and then at the bracelet in her hand. "I know it sounds stupid," she said reluctantly, "but I wanted to give the Greenwitch another secret to keep. Instead of the one we took. In my dream"— she paused, embarrassed, but went gamely on— "in my dream, I said, *I will give you another secret*, and the Greenwitch said in that big sad booming voice, '*Too late, too late*,' and just disappeared. . . ."

She was silent, gazing at the sea.

"I only said don't," Will said, "because I don't think your bracelet would really do. It's silver, isn't it, and the sea-water would turn it all black and dirty-looking."

"Oh," Jane said, forlorn.

Will shifted his footing on the wet rock, and felt in his pocket. He said, glancing briefly at Jane and then away, "I knew you'd want to give the Greenwitch something. I wondered if this would do."

Jane looked. Lying on Will's outstretched palm was the same small green-patched lead case that had held the manuscript, the Greenwitch's first secret. Will took it and pulled off the cap, shaking out a small object into her hand.

Jane saw a strip of yellow metal, gleaming, with some words engraved on it very small.

"It looks like gold," she said.

"It is," said Will. "Low carat, but gold. Last for ever, even down there."

Jane read out: *"Power from the green witch, lost beneath the sea."*

"That's just a line from a poem," Will said.

"Is it really? It's perfect." She ran her finger along the bright gold. "Where did you get it?"

"I made it."

"You made it?" Jane turned and stared at him with such astonishment that Will laughed.

"My father's a jeweller. He's teaching me to engrave things. I go and help in his shop sometimes after school."

"But you must have done this before you came down here, before you ever knew we were going to meet the Greenwitch," Jane said slowly. "How did you know what to make, what to write?"

"Just a lucky chance, I suppose," Will said, and there was a polite finality in his tone that reminded Jane instantly of Merriman: it was the voice that forbade any questioning.

"Oh," she said.

Will put the small golden strip into the case and fitted the cap on tightly. Then he handed it to her.

"Here's your secret, Greenwitch," Jane said, and she flung it into the sea. The little case vanished into the waves, their foam curling round the weed-fringed rocks. In the sunlight the water glittered like shattered glass.

"Thank you, Will Stanton," Jane said. She paused, looking at him. "You aren't quite like the rest of us, are you?"

"Not quite," said Will.

Jane said, "I hope we shall see you again, some day."

Will said, "I'm pretty sure you will."

*   *   *

Mr and Mrs Penhallow stood waving from the steps of the cottage, as they left: Merriman to put the four children on the London train, the Stantons on a visit to Truro for the day.

"Good-by!"

"Good journey to you! Good-by!"

The cars disappeared across the quay; overhead, sea gulls wheeled and cried.

"Perfessor did find what he came for, this time, I do believe," Mr Penhallow said, sucking pensively at his pipe.

"That liddle gold cup from last year, that was stole in London? Aye. But there was more, I fancy." Mrs Penhallow gazed at the point where Merriman's car had rounded the corner, with speculation in her eyes.

"More of what?"

" 'Twas no accident he came down here at Greenwitch time. He've never done that before. This was Cap'n Toms' first Greenwitch makin' at home for a good many years, too. . . . I don't know, Walter, I don't know. But something strange has been going on."

"You'm dreaming," Mr Penhallow said indulgently.

"That I'm not. But that young Jane was, one night. That same night everyone was dreaming, the night the whole village was hilla-ridden. . . . Such talk there was next morning, of things best forgotten. . . . And that morning, I was right near the bedrooms, going about my business, when young Jane woke up. And she let out such a hoot, and was out of her room like a wild thing running to her brothers."

"So she'd been dreaming, sure," Mr Penhallow said. "A bad 'un, by the sound of it. What of that?"

"Twasn't her dreaming that stays with me." Mrs Penhallow looked out at the quiet harbour, and the drifting gulls. " 'Twas her room. Clean as a pin it was the night before, she'm a neat little maid. But everywhere in that room, that morning, there was a great mess of little twigs and leaves, hawthorn leaves, and rowan. And everywhere a great smell of the sea."

*   *   *

Here ends GREENWITCH, *third book of the sequence named* THE DARK IS RISING. *The next book will be called* THE GREY KING. *There will be five books.*

A remarkable fantasy sequence by Susan Cooper, described by *The Horn Book* as being "as rich and eloquent as a Beethoven symphony."

The Dark Is Rising
A Newbery Honor Book
0-689-71087-9 (rack)
0-689-82983-3 (digest)

The Grey King
Winner of the Newbery Medal
0-689-71089-5 (rack)
0-689-82984-1 (digest)

Greenwitch
0-689-71088-7 (rack)
0-689-84034-9 (digest)

Silver on the Tree
0-689-71152-2 (rack)
0-689-84033-0 (digest)

Over Sea, Under Stone
0-02-042785-9 (rack)
0-689-84035-7 (digest)

The Dark Is Rising boxed set (includes all titles listed above)
0-02-042565-1

ALADDIN PAPERBACKS/SIMON & SCHUSTER CHILDREN'S PUBLISHING
www.SimonSaysKids.com

Aladdin Paperbacks is the place to come for top-notch fantasy/science-fiction! How many of these have *you* read?

The Tripods, by John Christopher

- ❑ Boxed Set • 0-689-00852-X
- ❑ The Tripods #1 *When the Tripods Came* • 0-02-042575-9
- ❑ The Tripods #2 *The White Mountains* • 0-02-042711-5
- ❑ The Tripods #3 *The City of Gold and Lead* • 0-02-042701-8
- ❑ The Tripods #4 *The Pool of Fire* • 0-02-042721-2

The Dark is Rising Sequence, by Susan Cooper

- ❑ Boxed Set • 0-02-042565-1
- ❑ *Over Sea, Under Stone* • 0-02-042785-9 (rack) • 0-689-84035-7 (digest)
- ❑ *The Dark Is Rising* • 0-689-71087-9 (rack) • 0-689-82983-3 (digest)
- ❑ *Greenwitch* • 0-689-71088-7 (rack) • 0-689-84034-9 (digest)
- ❑ *The Grey King* • 0-689-71089-5 (rack) • 0-689-82984-1 (digest)
- ❑ *Silver on the Tree* • 0-689-71152-2 (rack) • 0-689-84033-0 (digest)

The Dragon Chronicles, by Susan Fletcher

- ❑ *Dragon's Milk* • 0-689-71623-0
- ❑ *The Flight of the Dragon Kyn* • 0-689-81515-8
- ❑ *Sign of the Dove* • 0-689-82449-1

- ❑ *Virtual War*, by Gloria Skurzynski • 0-689-82425-4
- ❑ *Invitation to the Game*, by Monica Hughes • 0-671-86692-3

Aladdin Paperbacks
Simon & Schuster Children's Publishing
www.SimonSaysKids.com